"I'll walk you to your

"That isn't necessary," Libby said. "My cabin's right over there."

"Yes, but sometimes the coyotes come down from the hills at this hour," Matt insisted.

"But they wouldn't approach me, would they?"

"They might. I've heard they're partial to blondes in short skirts and fancy boots."

She broke into a smile. "I can fend them off. I'm tougher than I look."

"That's good. Because you look like a sugar cookie dipped in silver sprinkles."

"You don't like sugar cookies?"

"I never said I didn't like them. I can eat dozens of them." His amber eyes turned hungry. "I could even devour one whole."

Libby fidgeted in her seat. "You're making me nervous, Matt."

He dropped his gaze to her mouth. "I've been thinking about kissing you."

"You probably shouldn't be telling me this."

"I'm not taking it back, either. I admitted how I feel, and it's done and over now."

* * *

Wrangling the Rich Rancher is part of the Sons of Country series: Three heirs to country-music royalty face the music with three very special women...

Dear Reader,

When I suggested this series, focusing on a country star and his sons, I was thrilled that my editors liked the concept, too. I used to work for some famous musicians. Many years ago I painted the leather pick guards on the original Waylon Jennings signature guitars that the Fender Custom Shop produced. I painted the guitar straps that accompanied those guitars, too.

During that time I met Waylon backstage at a show, and he was just the nicest man. But by no means did I base this series on him. It doesn't have anything to do with Waylon Jennings or his family. Nonetheless, I've been inspired by having known so many interesting people in the music profession.

Truthfully, I'm actually more of a rock 'n' roll girl than a country gal, but many a country star has influenced me. For a short time I lived in Bakersfield, California, and I enjoyed going to Buck Owens Crystal Palace and checking out the memorabilia on the walls. I enjoyed listening to the music they played there, too. Is it any wonder I plotted a Sons of Country series? I think not.

Love and hugs,

Sheri WhiteFeather

SHERI WHITEFEATHER

—

WRANGLING
THE RICH RANCHER

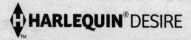

HARLEQUIN® DESIRE

Recycling programs
for this product may
not exist in your area.

ISBN-13: 978-0-373-83883-7

Wrangling the Rich Rancher

Copyright © 2017 by Sheree Henry-Whitefeather

This edition published by arrangement with Harlequin Books S.A.

For questions and comments about the quality of this book, please contact us at CustomerService@Harlequin.com.

Printed in U.S.A.

Sheri WhiteFeather is an award-winning, bestselling author. She writes a variety of romance novels for Harlequin and is known for incorporating Native American elements into her stories. She has two grown children, who are tribally enrolled members of the Muscogee Creek Nation. She lives in California and enjoys shopping in vintage stores and visiting art galleries and museums. Sheri loves to hear from her readers at sheriwhitefeather.com.

Books by Sheri WhiteFeather

Harlequin Desire

Billionaire Brothers Club

Waking Up with the Boss
Single Mom, Billionaire Boss
Paper Wedding, Best Friend Bride

Sons of Country

Wrangling the Rich Rancher

Visit her Author Profile page at Harlequin.com, or sheriwhitefeather.com, for more titles.

One

He was gorgeous, Libby Penn thought, this cowboy
she'd come to see. Yes, indeed: tall, dark and ruggedly
appealing, with a long, lean body, straight short black
hair and whiskey-colored eyes. All man, all denim and
leather, all Western. If she were in the market for a
lover, he would be darned hard to resist. But she hadn't
been with anyone since she'd lost her husband, and
she wasn't ready to sleep with Matt Clark or anyone
else. Not that Matt was asking her to share his bed.
She barely knew him. They'd only just met yesterday
afternoon, and briefly at that. Besides, she was here
for business, and she needed to keep her professional
wits about her.

Still, from the moment they'd first laid eyes on

each other, a strange sort of chemistry—the kind that zapped you when you least expected it—had risen up between them. Even now, she could sense his uneasy attraction to her, and he wasn't even looking her way. Clearly, he didn't like feeling something for one of his guests.

The thing was, she hadn't even told him the real reason she was here, staying at his recreational ranch. As far as he knew, she was just another tourist visiting the Texas Hill Country.

She and some of the other guests were finishing up breakfast, and soon would be dispersing to engage in whatever activities interested them: horseback riding, hiking, swimming, fishing, skeet shooting, horseshoes, Ping-Pong. There was a playground and petting corral for the kids. On top of that, the ranch had a world-class champion quarter horse standing at stud. They also bred him to their mares, and during foaling season, guests could ooh and aah over their offspring. Of course, hayrides, barbecues, campfires and country hoedowns were part of the regular program. According to the schedule she'd been given, a boot-scooting dance and fried chicken dinner were on the calendar for tomorrow night, with all ages welcome.

The Flying Creek Ranch was highly successful, earning plenty of cold, hard cash. Libby knew because she'd researched it. And although it was designed for families and looked quite rustic, there were luxurious undertones. Amid its vast and stunning acreage, it offered private cabin accommodations with limestone fireplaces. There was a big, beautiful main lodge, too, which was where Libby was now, preparing to approach Matt. But from what she'd gathered so far, Matt didn't live at the lodge. He lived in a cabin, the one next to hers, in fact. She'd spotted him last night, sitting quietly on his porch. She'd stayed inside, making notes to herself about Matt's character and how she perceived him. Friendly when he needed to be, but withdrawn, too. An enigma, she thought, a chameleon, his moods shifting with the summer wind.

Her observations were hasty at best, and influenced, no doubt, by what his father had already told her about him. Matt was Kirby Talbot's illegitimate son. The half-Cherokee boy the famous country singer had done wrong. Kirby had even written a yet-unpublished song about it.

Libby knew all sorts of personal details about Kirby. He'd hired her to write his biography. He'd handpicked her himself, based on a series of articles she'd crafted for *Rolling Stone*. For her, the book was a dream come true. Kirby was her idol, his rough-and-ready music complementing her willful personality and determined life.

Still studying Matt from across the room, she smoothed the front of her boho-inspired blouse, the silky fringe attached to it fluttering around her hips. The salesclerk at the store where she'd bought it called it cowgirl chic; it was bold, beautiful and sweetly feminine. Whatever the style, the blouse made her feel pretty. Libby was small in stature, with long, pale, wavy blond hair and a wholesome face. Sometimes she made cat eyes with her eyeliner just to doll herself up, giving her wide blue eyes a dramatic transformation.

Eager to learn more about Matt, she headed in his direction. Some of her research on him had come from his father and the rest from public records and the web. So far, she knew that he was thirty-one years old and had lived in the Hill Country his entire life. He appeared to be an unpretentious man, but his net worth was staggering, going far beyond the trust fund his father had set up for him.

As a youth, he'd excelled in junior rodeos. These days, he was divorced. His ex was a local girl, a widow when he'd married her, with two small children. That interested Libby, of course. But everything about him did.

He was Kirby's secret son. No one except the family and a handful of lawyers knew about him. After her book was released, everyone would know. Kirby wanted to come clean, to acknowledge Matt's paternity in a public way.

Initially, he'd kept Matt under wraps because he was married at the time and didn't want his wife or other kids to find out. Eventually they learned the truth. But that hadn't changed the dynamics of Matt and Kirby's relationship. He saw Matt sporadically when he was growing up, visiting between road tours. At some point, he stopped seeing him at all, and now Kirby wanted to make amends. Just this year, he started reaching out to his son, but Matt refused to take his calls, let alone see him.

Libby approached Matt, who was standing near a painting of Indian ponies dancing in the dust. He adjusted his hat, fitting it lower on his head.

"Do you have a minute?" she asked.

He turned more fully toward her, the make-believe horses prancing at his shoulder. "For one of my guests? Always."

"Is it okay if we take a walk?" She didn't want anyone to overhear their conversation. Some of the others were still milling around the lodge.

"Sure." He gestured to a side door leading to a rustic garden, where flowers sprouted amid wagon wheels, old water pumps and wrought iron benches. Once they were outside, he asked, "Is everything all right? Are you enjoying your stay so far?"

She fell into step with him. "It's a wonderful ranch, and I'm looking forward to the activities. I missed your Independence Day celebration." The ranch was famous for hosting a huge fireworks display, drawing crowds from neighboring communities. "You were booked solid then." She'd arrived just after July Fourth and would be staying until the beginning of August. "This is so different from where I live, so vast and rural." Libby was from Southern California, where she'd been born and raised. Kirby, however, resided in Nashville, on an enormous compound he'd built. She'd already been there several times. "My son will be joining me in a few weeks. My mother is going to bring him. She's going to stay with us, too."

"How old is your son?"

"Six. This place is going to thrill him. He wants to be a cowboy when he grows up."

He smiled a little crookedly. "I'll be sure to give him the grand tour."

"His daddy passed away. It'll be three years this fall." She wasn't sure why she felt inclined to tell Matt that, especially with how weirdly attracted to him she was. Then again, he'd been married to a widow, so maybe he would understand more than most people would?

By now, he was frowning, hard and deep. "I'm sorry for your loss."

"Thank you. His name was Becker." Kirby Talbot had been his idol, too. She'd met Becker at one of Kirby's concerts. "He got sick. But it happened really quickly. A bacterial infection that…" She let her words drift. Becker wouldn't want her talking about the way he died. He was a vibrant person, filled with hope and joy. "But this isn't what I intended to discuss with you." She managed a smile, knowing Becker would be encouraging her to move forward, especially with her career. Then, suddenly, she hesitated, fully aware that Matt wasn't going to be pleased with her news. Finally, she slapped the smile back on her face and went for it. "I'm doing a book about your father. He hired me to write his biography, and—"

"Kirby sent you here?" Matt flinched, his amber eyes flashing beneath the brim of his straw Stetson.

She nodded. "He asked me to come. He wants to reveal your parentage in the book and wants to give you the opportunity to tell your side of the story."

Anger edged his voice. "So you're here to interview me?"

She nodded again, maintaining a professional air. Libby wasn't going to let Matt's frustration affect her. She had a job to do, a biography to write, possibly even bringing him and his father together. "I'd like the chance to get to know you, to spend as much time with you as I can. Kirby told me—"

"He told you what?" Those eyes flashed again. "That his bastard son wants nothing to do with him?"

"He didn't word it like that, but yes, he said that you were estranged from him. But he also admitted how he'd done you wrong. How he was never really there for you when you were growing up. He wants to atone for his mistakes."

A cynical smile thinned Matt's lips. "So it'll make him look good in the book you're writing? So his fans can worship him more than they already do?" Tall and handsome and lethal, he took a step closer to her. "You can tell my arrogant, womanizing daddy to go straight to hell. That I'm not impressed with him or his half-assed biography."

Half-assed? Libby set her chin. "I'm going to write a true account of his life, his loves, his mistakes, his music. His children," she added. Kirby had two other sons, legitimate heirs with his former wife, the woman to whom he'd been married when Matt's mother had tumbled into an affair with him. "From my understanding, you've never even met your brothers."

"My *half* brothers," he reminded her. "And I'm not any more interested in them than I am in Kirby."

"They're interested in you."

He shifted his booted feet. "They told you that?"

"Yes, they did." They were willing participants in the book. "I haven't interviewed them yet, not extensively, but we've had a couple of nice talks where they expressed their desire to meet you." He was the lone-wolf brother they couldn't help but wonder about. "Brandon is an entertainment lawyer who represents the family, and Tommy…" She paused. "Well, he's a lot like Kirby."

Matt raised his eyebrows. "You think I don't know that? I'm familiar with Tommy Talbot's music. I know how he followed in our old man's footsteps."

Yes, she thought. Tommy was as wild as their father. Or wilder, if that was possible. Whereas Kirby had been dubbed the bad boy of country, Tommy was now known as the *baddest* boy of country, surpassing his father.

She said, "If you agree to do this, I promise that I'll quote you accurately, that I'll present you in a deep and honest light. Your words matter. Your thoughts, your feelings. I'm hoping to interview your mother, as well." Libby knew that his mom lived on the ranch. "She just got married, didn't she? To a man who works for you?"

"Yes, but they're out of town right now." He moved even closer to her, so close their boot tips were almost touching. "So you can't go chasing after her for an interview."

"That's okay. I can wait." He towered over her and Libby lifted her head to get a better look at him. This close, he was even more appealing, his features etched in masculine lines and candid emotion. He smelled good, too, his cologne a tantalizing blend of woods and musk.

"Has he hit on you yet?"

She started. "I'm sorry. What?"

"Kirby. Has he tried to get you into bed?"

"Oh, my goodness, no." Discomfort blasted through her blood. It was the son who stirred her, not the father. "He's been nothing but respectful to me."

"Are you sure?" he asked, his voice going a tad too soft. In it, she heard a gentle concern, a protective tone.

"I'm positive." She knew that Kirby wasn't interested in her. If anything, he'd been paternal toward her. But she decided not to mention that to Matt, given how easily Kirby had once walked away from him.

He went silent, and his gaze locked onto hers. Then, as if suddenly realizing how close he was standing to her, he stepped back.

"Sorry," he said.

"You don't have to apologize. I rather liked it." She tried for a goofy smile. "This noble side of you."

He remained serious. "If my dad got a hold of you, he would destroy your soul. You and your naive ways."

And what would Matt do if he got a hold of her? "There's nothing going on with your father and me. I don't feel that way about him." She closed the gap between them, wanting to be near him again. "And I'm not as naive as I look."

"Oh, yeah. So what are you going to do, little girl? Seduce me for the sake of your book?"

Mercy, she thought. Were they actually having this conversation? Was it really going in this direction? Struggling to breathe, to keep the air in her lungs from rushing out, she said, "If I seduced you, it wouldn't be for the sake of the book." She quickly clarified, "But I'm not here to seduce anyone. And for the record, I'm not a little girl. I'm twenty-nine."

His gaze didn't falter, not one whiskey inch. "I'll keep that in mind."

He would keep what in mind? Her self-proclaimed maturity? Or her unwillingness to seduce anyone? Either way, she was still feeling a bit too breathless. "Are you going to grant me an interview? Are you going to agree to spend some time with me? Or am I going to have to keep trying to convince you to be part of my project?"

"You'll have to keep trying. For all the good it will do you."

"It'll do me plenty of good." This was her first book, and she intended to do it right.

"Then I guess I'll see you around." He sent her a pulse-jarring look, right before he walked away, leaving her staring after him.

Like a fresh-faced schoolgirl with a crush.

* * *

Matt cursed the situation he was in. Of all the beautiful blondes who could have shown up at his ranch, did it have to be someone who was working for his dad? Someone who was prying into the past? Who was writing a book that was going to unmask the chaos in his life? The last thing Matt wanted was to be publically identified as Kirby Talbot's son. Damn his dad all to hell.

And damn Libby, too.

Yesterday when she arrived, Matt had gotten a hot, sexy, zipper-tightening reaction to her. So much so, he'd given her the cabin next to his. Normally he didn't work the front desk or place his guests. But he'd just happened to be there when she'd come in, so he'd handled the transaction.

Honestly, though, he didn't know what he was trying to accomplish by putting her next to him. For all he knew, she could have been in a relationship. Sure, she seemed single from the way she'd been checking him out, but he knew better than to lust after one of his guests.

Cripes, he thought. Besides being his father's biographer, she was widowed with a kid. This was the nightmare of nightmares. He'd gotten his heart broken by the last widow, the last blonde, who caught his eye. He missed Sandy. He missed her children, too. Two adorable little twins girls.

Matt had wanted so desperately to be a father—a

good, kind, caring dad to Sandy's girls. He wanted to give them what his old man had never given him.

Love. Affection. Attention.

But after the divorce, she'd taken the twins and moved out of the area. She didn't think it would be healthy for her or the girls to keep seeing him. Sandy had only married him to soothe the loss of the man she really loved. The guy she'd buried.

How was he supposed to compete with that? Sandy's memories of her other husband had always been there, floating like a ghost between them. Matt's mixed-up marriage, which lasted all of six months, had been a crushing failure. He thought that he could help Sandy through her grief, that he would become her hero and the new husband she couldn't live without.

A year had passed since the divorce, and just as he was starting to lick to his wounds and move on, in walked another young widow, except she was working for his dad.

Oh, yeah. This was a nightmare, all right. Was he supposed to avoid Libby while she was here, to walk away from her at every turn? Considering how long she would be hanging around, that wasn't going to be an easy feat.

He could ask her to leave. This was his ranch, after all—he'd started the business from a trust account Kirby had set up for him. Of course, it wasn't as cut-and-dried as that. After Matt got the ranch established, making it a tremendous success, he returned the money to the trust, making sure his dad knew that he no longer needed or wanted it. By now, Matt was wealthy in his own right.

Initially, he'd acquired a lump sum on his twenty-first birthday, based on a deal that had been negotiated when he was a baby, as part of a child-support settlement. His mom had agreed to the terms, which required her to keep Matt's paternity a secret.

Disturbing as it was, the contract had never restricted Kirby from speaking out. Only Matt's mother had been silenced, and she'd taught Matt to stay silent, as well, to never tell anyone who his father was. And now, all these years later, Kirby wanted to blow all that out of the water.

Matt headed to his private barn, preparing to saddle one of his horses and ride into the hills, taking a trail that was unavailable to his guests. He often carved out time for himself, and today in particular he wasn't in the mood to socialize, not with what Libby had sprung on him.

Unfortunately, when his mom returned from her trip, she would probably support this damned book. She'd already been encouraging Matt to make peace with his father, to accept the olive branches Kirby had been offering.

He kept walking, and just as he entered his barn, he turned and saw Libby strolling up behind him.

Holy hell.

Half annoyed, half intrigued and a whole lot confused, he let his gaze roam over her. She'd actually followed him out here, and without him even knowing it. "When I said that I would see you around, I didn't mean this soon."

"Really, you didn't? Oh, silly me." She grinned, two perfect dimples lighting up her face.

He wanted to grab her by that fringy top of hers and shake her till those dimples rattled. But he wanted to kiss her, too, as roughly as he could, curious to know if she tasted as feisty as she looked.

"Yeah, silly you," he shot back.

She was still grinning, still being cute and clever. "I'm prone to getting the last word, and you left me standing there like a dolt."

He had no idea what that meant. "A dolt?"

"A stupid person."

Matt was the stupid one, wishing he could kiss her. "Working for Kirby doesn't exactly make you the brightest bulb in the chandelier."

"Funny, I'm wearing chandelier earrings, and they're pretty bright." She tapped the crystal jewels at her ears. "I made them myself."

Way to change the subject, he thought, enticed by how sparkly she was. "Okay, so you got the last word. Will you leave me alone now?"

"Nope." She spun around in a pretty little pirouette, making her fringe fly. "I think you should dance with me."

He blinked at her. "You want me to two-step with you? Here? Now?"

"No. Tomorrow night." She glanced down at her

feet. Her silver glitter boots were as flashy as her earrings. "At the hoedown."

Right. The weekly barn dance at the ranch. "I don't always go to those." Sometimes he preferred to stay home, letting his guests kick up their heels without him. "And dancing with you sounds like a dolt of a thing to do."

"Come on. Take a chance."

He wasn't making any promises, especially to her. "I might show up, and I might not. But just so you know, the house band isn't allowed to play Kirby's music. Or Tommy's, either. So don't get smart and make any requests."

"I won't. But doesn't the band wonder why the Talbots are off-limits? Or why they have to turn down requests for their songs?"

"My ranch. My rules. And there are plenty of other artists they cover. Traditional, bluegrass, honky-tonk, alternative, outlaw. They play it all." Except for the badass Talbots. Their brand of outlaw twisted Matt's gut.

She bounced in her boots. "Dancing with you is going to be fun. Think how easily we're going to become friends." She teased him, "Or frenemies, if you prefer."

"I just told you that I might not be there."

"Personally, I don't think you're going to be able to resist. I'm the most persuasive cowgirl you're ever going to meet."

"You're not a cowgirl. You're a chick from Hermosa

Beach who wears fancy Western clothes and dotes on my ass-hat of a father."

She laughed, obviously amused by his assessment of her. He knew where she was from because when he'd checked her into the ranch, he'd seen her driver's license, with her name, her address, her birth date. He already knew she was twenty-nine, even before she told him how old she was.

"You have a wicked sense of humor, Matt."

"I wasn't trying to be funny."

"That's just my point."

He squared his shoulders. "I'm going riding now, and you're not coming with me. So whatever you do, don't follow me into the hills."

Her dimples twitched. "We'll save that for another time. Only I won't be following you. You're going to like me enough that you'll be inviting me to join you."

"Gee, humble much?" This wannabe cowgirl was hell on wheels. And the crazy part was, he already liked her, even if he didn't want to.

She laughed again. "See, there you go. Funny, but not trying to be. Enjoy your ride, and I'll see you tomorrow night."

One last smile, and she exited the barn, taking her last words with her. And damn if he wasn't tempted to teach her a lesson. And leave her dancing all by her beautiful self.

Two

Libby stood in front of the mirror, putting the final touches on her outfit. Soon she would be leaving for the dance. She planned to walk to the barn where the soiree was being held. From her cabin, the path was well lit and paved with stones. She could have called ahead and gotten a ride from a lodge attendant. The ranch offered a shuttle service, taking guests to and from activities. But she intended to bask in the night air, enjoying the sights and scents along the way.

She returned her gaze to the mirror. She was wearing a short, sassy skirt and the same boots and earrings Matt had already seen before.

What he'd said about her was true. She wasn't a cowgirl, at least not in the literal sense of the word.

She didn't herd cattle or compete in rodeos. But she loved all things country, especially the music.

She didn't mind being a chick from Hermosa Beach who wore fancy Western clothes. She was proud to own that identity. But had she gone too far, baiting Matt to dance with her? At the time it had seemed like a good way to create a friendly rapport between them. Only now, as the opportunity drew near, she was nervous about seeing him.

Nervous about how he made her feel.

Granted, Libby kept telling herself that she wasn't ready for a lover, but the thought of being with him kept crossing her mind, making her warm all over.

She'd never slept with anyone except Becker, so the idea of seducing Matt seemed almost laughable. But it seemed hot and wild and exciting, too. Too wild? Too exciting? Even if she had the guts to do it, being with Matt would complicate an already complicated situation, jumbling her plans to interview him. Then why did she keep thinking about him in sexual ways? Why did sleeping with him keep invading her thoughts?

Maybe it would be better if he ditched her tonight, if he didn't show up. Or maybe she should bail out.

Oh, right. Like that wouldn't make her look like an idiot, after the overly confident way she'd presented herself. No. Libby was going to see this through. She was going to march into that place with a big, bright smile on her face.

She ventured onto her porch and glanced over at Matt's cabin. She assumed he wasn't home because his truck wasn't parked in the gravel driveway. Was he at the hoedown already? Or had he gone somewhere else instead?

She took a second glance at his cabin. It appeared to be the same two-bedroom model as hers. Was that where he'd always lived, even during his short-lived marriage? Or had he been planning to build a bigger place on his property? It struck her odd that he chose to live in a modest cabin when he could have a mansion if he wanted one. There was no way to know why he did what he did, except to ask him. Kirby certainly wasn't privy to that information. What he knew about his son could fill a thimble.

Libby locked her cabin and left for the dance. By the time she arrived, the big wooden building was filled with people—adults and children—eating and drinking and being merry.

The decor was charmingly Western, with twinkling lights streaming from the rafters, red-and-white tablecloths and folding chairs upholstered in cowhide.

The band hadn't taken the stage yet, but they would probably appear soon enough.

She looked around for Matt. He was nowhere to be seen. Keeping herself busy, she wandered over to the buffet and filled her plate. She took a seat at one of the tables, chatted with other guests and dived into her meal.

The fried chicken was to die for and the mashed potatoes were even better. She didn't go back for dessert. She was already getting full.

An hour passed. By then the band was playing, and people were line dancing, laughing, clapping and missing steps. Of course some of them were right on the money. Libby was a good dancer, too. But at this point she was standing in a corner like a wallflower, watching the festivities.

Okay, so maybe Matt wasn't coming. Maybe he didn't find her, or her spunky personality, as irresistible as she assumed he would.

Served her right, she supposed. But suddenly something inside her felt far too alone, far too widowed. She didn't like being here without a partner.

She toyed with her empty ring finger. She'd removed her wedding band about a year after Becker passed, but now she wished she'd kept it on.

Still, she knew better than to wallow in sadness. She'd worked hard to overcome her grief.

Should she get out there and dance? Should she join the party on her own? Or should she give Matt a little more time, in case he decided to materialize?

"Have you been waiting for me?" a raspy voice whispered in her ear from behind her.

Matt. It was him. Talk about materializing, and at the perfect moment, too. But she was reluctant to turn around, afraid that he would disappear as mysteriously as he'd arrived.

"I knew you'd come," she said, lying through her teeth.

"Oh, yeah?" Still standing behind her, he gripped

her waist. "Then let's dance." As quick as could be, he spun her around to face him.

Making her heart spin, too.

Matt and Libby danced for hours. They did fancy two-steps and three-steps. They country waltzed, line danced and did the push, the Cotton Eye Joe and the schottische.

The fast dances were easy for Matt. The slow ones, not so much. He had to hold Libby closer for those.

Like now. The band was doing a cover of Lady Antebellum's "Can't Take My Eyes Off You," with lyrics about a woman's devotion to her partner.

"I love this song," Libby said, sounding a little dreamy.

Matt didn't comment on the music. He was doing his damnedest not to press his body even closer to hers. This wasn't a sexy setting, and he couldn't misbehave, not here, not like this. Not at all, he warned himself.

Her hair, he noticed, smelled like lemons, and her cheeks were flushed with a healthy glow. Did she surf and swim and do all those California-girl-type things? Did she go to beach parties with her friends or walk barefoot through the sand at night? He was as curious about her as she was about him.

But he wasn't writing a book that would damage her. He wasn't doing anything except getting distracted by her nearness, lowering his guard with a woman who wanted to invade his privacy.

She looked up at him. "Things are starting to wind down."

He slid his hand a bit lower on her back. "The parents usually take their little ones back to their cabins or rooms by now. But not everyone has kids. Some of the couples who come to the ranch are honeymooners. Some are long-married seniors, too." He stopped and adjusted his hand, returning it to a more proper position. But it didn't help. He was still struggling with her proximity. "We don't get many single folks."

"Like me?"

"You're not a regular guest."

She followed his lead, moving in sync with him. "No, but I'm still a real person."

Too real, he thought, too warm and pliable in his arms. Now all he wanted was for the song to end. Finally, it did, leaving him with a knot in his chest. The last time he'd danced this close to a woman was with Sandy, when he'd still believed he could make his marriage work.

He hastily asked, "Do you want to go outside and catch a breath of air?"

"Why? Do you think it's getting warm in here?"

"Warm enough." He needed to stop holding Libby, to stop swaying to romantic songs. But more ballads were on the way. He knew the band's set.

He escorted her onto the patio, where hay bales draped in blue gingham served as seats. They sat next to each other in a secluded spot. He glanced up at the starry sky, then shifted his gaze back to her. She was as bright as the night, with her silver boots and shimmery earrings.

As she settled onto the hay bale she adjusted the hem of her skirt, keeping it from riding farther up her thighs. It made Matt wonder what she had going on under that flouncy garment. Cute little bikini panties? A seductive thong? Whatever her undies were, they were none of his business.

None whatsoever.

"I almost stood you up," he said. "I went to the local watering hole before I came here, and that's where I was going to stay. But I changed my mind." He hadn't even finished his beer. He'd just tipped the gnarly old bartender and left. "I guess I wanted to see if you'd be waiting for me."

"Truthfully?" She tugged at her hem again. "I started to worry that you might leave me hanging."

"So you're not as self-assured as you claim to be?" To him, she still seemed like a force to be reckoned with.

"Mostly I am. Only with you, I wasn't sure what to expect. But it worked out nicely, I think."

"What did? Us dancing together?"

"Yep." She smiled, disarming him with her dimples.

He turned away, staring into the distance, the darkness. Sandy's smile wasn't as girlish as Libby's. She didn't have blue eyes, either. Hers were a brownish hazel. Aside from being blondes, they didn't look that much alike. But they had other things in common, like the way they made him feel. That, and the fact that they were both widows.

He returned his gaze to hers. "You should have never come to my ranch, sneaking in, pretending to be a guest."

"How else was I supposed to get to know you? If I would have called ahead and told you who I was and what my agenda was, you wouldn't have agreed to see me."

"You're right. I wouldn't have." He paused, then asked, "Have you been to Kirby's place? Or Kirbyville, as everyone calls it."

"Yes. It's a spectacular compound. That's where I'll be going when I leave here. He wants you to visit him there, too."

"So he keeps saying." Matt couldn't stand the thought of her going back to his dad. "Now that you're here, I'm not going to send you away. I considered it, but it didn't seem right, somehow."

"Thank you. You're a fascinating man. You intrigued me from the start."

"You wouldn't be saying that if I wasn't Kirby's bastard."

She frowned. "Why do you keep calling yourself that?"

"Because that's what I am. And it's how Kirby always made me feel, sweeping me under the carpet when I was a kid. He never even—" Matt hesitated, stopping himself from opening up more than he already had. "I shouldn't be talking to you about this, giving you material for your book."

"I can't just take our conversations and use them, not without getting a signed release from you. The publisher is being very strict about that. I need to interview you properly, to record you and quote you accurately."

She expected to record him? Fat chance of that. "So anything we say without the release is off the record?"

"Yes. But if you don't let me interview you, everything in the book that pertains to you will come from Kirby or your brothers or whoever else mentions you. That's all I'll be able to write about you."

"I don't want you writing about me at all." How many times did he have to tell her that? "I just want to be left alone."

She replied in a gentle tone, "This book is an amazing opportunity for me, and I'm going to write it, no matter what. But my heart is in the right place. I'm not trying to hurt or sensationalize you."

"It sure seems that way to me. The sensationalize part, anyway." He didn't think that she'd set out to hurt him, even if her actions would be doing just that. "Do you know the mess Kirby's biography is going to make of my life? I won't have any privacy after my paternity is revealed."

"It'll cause some attention at first, but Kirby said he'll hire a PR team to help you manage it. He doesn't expect you to weather it by yourself."

"Gee, how gracious of him."

"I understand that you're angry about the way he

treated you. But your paternity shouldn't have been kept a secret to begin with. If Kirby had acknowledged you from the beginning, you would already be known as his son."

"That's a moot point all these years later. If he wanted to be my father, he should have manned up back then." Matt didn't have any patience for his dad's newfound interest in him. His old man should have forewarned him about the book, too, instead of sending a pretty little writer to do it.

She went silent, letting him brood. A moment later, she said, "I was thinking of taking a shuttle into town tomorrow, then renting a car while I'm there. Unless you'd be willing to drive me. You could be my guide."

"Sorry, but I'm going to pass." He didn't want to show her around his hometown. He figured that she just wanted to go there to try to learn more about where he'd grown up. "But I'd be glad to escort you back to your cabin now."

"The dance isn't even over yet."

"It's getting close. This is the last song." He could hear the music drifting outside. "They always end with a Texas waltz."

"It sure is pretty."

As pretty as it got, he supposed. Just like her. "So, do you want me to give you a ride back to your cabin?"

She tucked a strand of her lemony hair behind her ear. "Sure, I'll go with you." She lifted her feet off the ground, tipping her toes to the sky. "It'll make me feel like a rodeo queen, riding beside the handsomest cowboy in the land."

"You wish." He stood and extended a hand. "And calling me handsome isn't going to boost your cause."

She accepted his hand and let him help her up. "Are you sure about that?"

"Yeah." Nothing was going to take the sting out of her writing Kirby's biography. Except maybe sweeping her into a mindless kiss that would make him forget his worries. Or reaching his hand under her skirt. Or hauling her off, like a caveman, to his bed. But he wasn't going to do any of those things.

No matter how good they would make him feel.

When Matt pulled into his driveway and parked, Libby was still thinking about the book and how she was going to get him to agree to be part of it. But as they turned toward each other, a strange sensation came over her—almost as if they were on a date and she was going home with him for the very first time.

He frowned, and she suspected the same awkward notion had come over him. The porch light from his cabin created a misty glow, intensifying the ambience.

Neither of them spoke. Not a word. Until he said, "Don't worry. I'll walk you to your door."

"That isn't necessary." She'd walked to the dance by herself. So why would she need an escort now? "My cabin is just right over there."

"Yes, but sometimes the coyotes come down from

the hills at this hour. We've got lots of them around here."

"But they wouldn't approach me, would they?" She couldn't imagine it.

"They might." He spoke in a serious tone. "I've heard they're partial to blondes in short skirts and fancy boots."

She broke into a smile, grateful for his offbeat sense of humor. She knew now that he was kidding. "I can fend them off. I'm tougher than I look."

"That's good." He chuckled. "Because you look like a sugar cookie dipped in silver sprinkles."

She feigned offense. "You don't like sugar cookies? What kind of crazy person are you?"

"I never said I didn't like them." His humor faded. "I can eat dozens of them." His amber eyes turned hungry. "I could even devour one whole."

Libby fidgeted in her seat. If she were smart, she would make an off-the-cuff remark. She would crack a joke. But she didn't do anything except sit there like the cookie in question.

She finally drummed up the courage to say, "You're making me nervous, Matt." She didn't usually admit defeat, but her defensive mechanism was on the blink, screws and bolts coming loose.

He stared at her mouth. A second later, he lifted his gaze back to her face, snaring her in his trap.

"I've been thinking about kissing you," he said. "I'm not going to do it, but I keep thinking about it."

"You probably shouldn't be telling me this." Just as

she shouldn't be imagining how his kiss would feel—hot and wild, with his hands tangled in her hair, his tongue slipping past her lips.

"I even wondered about what kind of panties you have on."

Embarrassed by his admission, by the shameful thrill it gave her, she pressed her knees together. "I'm not going to tell you."

"I'm not asking you to. But I'm not taking it back, either. I admitted how I feel, and it's over and done with now."

It wasn't over for her. She wanted to know more about him, so much more. "Have you been playing around since your divorce?" she asked, curious about his habits, his primal needs. "Do you go to the bar to meet women?"

He scowled at her. "You have no right to ask me that."

"After the things you said to me, I think I'm entitled to a little payback." She was still pinning her knees together, still feeling the discomfort of being the cookie he wanted to devour.

He cursed quietly.

She went flippant. "Is that a yes or a no? I couldn't quite tell."

He almost laughed. But he almost snarled, too. The sound that erupted from him was as unhinged as their attraction.

"If I'd been getting laid," he said, "would I be acting like a rutting bull around you?"

"I don't know," she challenged him, determined to get a straight answer. "Would you?"

He shook his head. "You're something else, Libby."

She was just trying to make being the object of his desire more bearable, even if meant getting him to admit that he'd been alone since his divorce. "Maybe I better go home now."

"Back to California?"

Big, handsome jerk. "Back to my cabin."

"Damn. I should have known you wouldn't cut bait and run."

"You don't have to walk me to my door." Now that she knew there weren't any coyotes out to get her. "You don't have to play the gentleman."

"I wasn't playing at anything. But it's probably better if I keep my distance. I'd just want to kiss you, and that'll only make things worse."

She wasn't sure if they could get any worse. He was already making her far too weak. If he kissed her at her door, she would probably melt at his feet.

He said, "You should go home for real."

She refused to concede, to get any weaker than she already was. "Sorry, cowboy, but you're stuck with me."

He leaned back against the seat, as if he were weary. Or lonely. Or something along those lines.

He sat forward again. "Maybe I will take you into town tomorrow."

Her pulse bumped a beat. "Really?"

"Sure. Why not? There's a bakery where we can get some cookies."

She laughed even if she shouldn't have. "You've got a hankering, do you?"

"Hell, yes. Don't you?"

More than he could possibly know. "Will you show me the house where you grew up?" It was at the top of her list of places to see. She had the address, but she hadn't run a map on it yet.

"I suppose I could take you. It's better than you poking around out there alone."

She eagerly asked, "Is this the start of us being friends?"

"I think it's more like the other thing you said we could become."

"Frenemies?"

"That's it. I'll pick you up tomorrow around two. I have some work to do on the ranch before then. But for now, we both need to get some sleep."

Yes, they did, she thought, each of them in his or her own bed. "I'll see you." Libby bid him a hasty goodbye, opened the passenger's-side door and darted off, clinging to the shadows, trying to be less visible. She sensed that he was watching every move she made.

Was he still thinking sexy thoughts? Did he wish that he'd kissed her? That he'd pulled her body close to his? That he'd put his mouth all over hers?

She ascended her porch steps without glancing back. Self-conscious, she fumbled putting the key in the lock. She went inside, and as soon as she closed the door, she crept over to the living room window and peered through the blinds.

Matt remained in his truck, a lone figure behind the wheel.

She kept spying on him, holding her breath, anxious to see him walk to his door. He finally got out of the vehicle, taking long determined strides. She watched, absorbed by his rugged movements, breathless for every dizzying moment until he entered his cabin and turned on his lights.

Leaving her alone in the dark.

The next afternoon, Libby waited on her porch for Matt. She'd dressed down a bit, wearing a plaid shirt, blue jeans and a pair of traditional brown boots. Of course, her belt buckle was shiny and so was her jewelry. She never left the house without a touch of glamour.

She removed her phone from her purse and checked the time. Matt wasn't late, but he was cutting it close. And now, in the light of day, with nothing between them except last night's convoluted hunger, she was concerned that he might cancel their outing.

She frowned at her phone. They hadn't even exchanged numbers. She couldn't text him to see if he was on his way.

He hadn't told her what type of work he had to do on the ranch today, and when she'd awakened this morning his truck was already gone. She hadn't seen him at the lodge during breakfast or lunch, either.

Funny how she missed him already. She'd known him all of three days, and her interactions with him were shaky, at best. There was no logic in missing him.

Missing Becker made sense.

She kept tons of pictures of her late husband on her phone. Her son loved looking at them. He adored chatting about his daddy and asking Libby questions about him. Chance was three when Becker died. He didn't have many memories to rely on.

She plopped down on a barrel chair to wait for Matt. She hadn't mentioned her son's name to him. Maybe she would do that today. Of course, she doubted that Matt was going to like that she'd named her son Chance Mitchell after a fictitious character, a legendary outlaw, in one of Kirby's most famous songs.

She looked up and saw Matt's truck. It appeared out of a cloud of dust, and she popped up from her seat. The man certainly knew how to make an entrance.

She glanced at her phone before she put it away. He was right on time. Not a minute late, not a second early. Somehow he managed to get there at 2:00 p.m. on the dot.

He pulled into her driveway and kept the engine running. She raced down the porch steps, her hair flying. She'd washed it this morning with her latest favorite shampoo. She changed her toiletries nearly as often as she changed her clothes. She liked trying new products. She wasn't nearly as adventurous about trying new men. Yet here she was, getting swept away by Matt.

She climbed into his truck, and he said, "Hey, Libby."

"Hey, yourself." She noticed that his hat was sitting in the back seat, as it were along for the ride.

Off they went, with the sun shining in the Texas sky. She gazed out the window, watching the landscape go by. The drive was long and scenic, with roads that wound through the hills.

"This is the back way," he said.

"I gathered as much." They weren't on the main highway that led to and from the ranch.

In the next bout of silence, she studied Matt's appearance. His hair looked mussed, spiky in spots from where he'd probably dragged his hands through it. He seemed dangerous, forbidden. But why wouldn't he, with the way he made her feel? Last night she'd slept with her bedroom window open, letting the breeze drift over her half-clothed body. She'd gone to bed wearing the panties he'd wondered about. She'd even touched herself, sliding her fingers past the waistband and down into the fabric, fantasizing that he was doing it.

Matt shot her a quick glance, and her cheeks went horribly hot. He couldn't know what she'd been thinking, but she reacted as if he did.

"You okay?" he asked.

Not in the least, she thought. "I'm fine."

"You're usually more talkative."

She adjusted the air-conditioning vent on her side,

angling it to get a stronger flow. "You don't know me well enough to say what I usually do."

"All right, then. Based on my experiences with you, you're usually more talkative."

"I'm just enjoying the ride."

"You don't seem like you are. What are you thinking about?"

She couldn't stand the tension that was building inside her. And now she wanted him to suffer, too. He was being too danged casual. "That they were pink."

"What?"

"My panties. They were pink, low-rise hipsters, silk, with a see-through lace panel in front."

He nearly lost his grip on the wheel, and she felt a whole lot better. She even managed to toss a "got ya" grin at him.

"Don't you flash your dimples at me, woman. You could have gotten us killed."

"Over an itty-bitty pair of panties? You're a better driver than that."

He focused on looking out the windshield.

She tortured him some more. "I have a similar pair on now. Only they're blue."

His breath went choppy. "I'm going to strangle you. I swear I am."

"I'm just getting you in the mood for the cookie you were hankering for."

"Knock it off." He took a bend in the road. "Just stop yapping about it."

She sat smugly in her seat, grateful her tactic had

worked. She needed to take charge, to feel strong and powerful in his presence. "You wanted me to be more talkative."

"You think I'm kidding about strangling you?" His tone turned feral. "Or maybe I ought to kiss you instead."

Oh, my God. Now she'd gone and done it. She'd awakened the predator in him. His lips, she noticed, were twisted into a snarl. "You look more like you're going to bite me."

"That'll work, too. But I'm not going to do either."

Libby didn't know whether to be relieved or disappointed. Her heart was practically leaping out of her chest.

"We're almost there," he said, changing the subject.

"Almost where?"

"At my old house. You asked to see it."

"It's way out here?" She'd assumed it was on the outskirts of town, but she hadn't expected it to be this far out.

He veered onto a dirt road, and she craned her neck to get a better look. A lovely stone house, a miniranch of sorts, sat in a canyon all by itself.

He stopped at the top of the road, where a private gate blocked them from going any farther.

"Who lives there now?" she asked.

"The people Mom rents it to. They raise paint horses. We had a little breeding farm, too. Mom called it Canyon Farms then."

"It's so isolated."

"Kirby built it for Mom when I was a baby." His tone turned pensive. "Mom was originally from Austin, and her parents had passed away about three years before, so she was alone, except for me. She liked this area. Her folks used to bring her here on camping trips. It held nice memories for her. So when Kirby offered to buy her a place, she asked him if it could be in Creek Hill."

"Did she want to be this far from town?" Libby glanced around again. "Just the two of you, in the middle of a canyon?"

"Not necessarily. It was Kirby who chose this location, so he could visit without anyone seeing him coming and going. It was mostly at night since that's the schedule he was used to keeping. It continued on that way, even as I got older. I remember how Mom would fuss over him on the nights he came by, as if he was royalty." Matt made a disgusted sound. "What did he tell you about his relationship with my mother?"

"He said that she's the longest mistress he ever had. That it ended when you were around twelve." A clandestine affair for over a decade, she thought. Libby couldn't fathom subjecting herself to something like that. But it wasn't her place to judge Kirby or Matt's mother or anyone else.

"She was foolish enough to remain faithful to him, even when she knew that he had other mistresses or girlfriends or whatever. And then there was his wife and other children. The family he was protecting." Matt's expression went taut. "In the beginning I didn't know he was my father. Mom just told me that he was her friend. I was too young to recognize him or know that he was famous." He roughly added, "I'm not telling you this so you can feel bad for me. I'm telling you because I want you to know the kind of man Kirby really is, to get a better idea of who you're working for."

"I know who he is." She wasn't going to hold Kirby's mistakes against him, not when he was trying, with all of his heart, to repair the damage he'd done. "And I know how badly he wants to make amends with you."

Matt squinted at her. "I started to suspect that he was my dad even before Mom told me that he was. This tall, bearded man in a long black duster, this larger-than-life guy. He never got up before noon, but Mom would still cook him breakfast food, treating the afternoons as if they were mornings. Sometimes he would even sit at the table with his sunglasses on. I'd never seen anyone do that indoors before. I knew he was different from other people. I just didn't know how different. But either way, he was just too important to my mother, too revered, I figured, for him to be someone other than my father. Once I learned the truth, I accepted it as the status quo."

"You must have been a highly observant child."

"Yes, but I was ridiculously impressionable, too. Kirby told me once that I looked like I was part wolf, and I figured my eyes were this color because I was supposed to be nocturnal, the way he was. But I'd get so sleepy when he first arrived at night and I was waiting up to see him. I didn't understand how I could be part wolf if I couldn't stay up at night."

"Your eyes are beautiful." Mesmerizing, she thought. Hypnotizing. She could stare at them for hours.

He scoffed at her compliment. "They're weird, and you're missing my point."

"No, I'm not." She understood what he was trying to convey. How lonely Kirby had made him feel. How he needed to be part of the daylight, where fathers took their sons out in public, where there were no secrets, where normalcy existed. "It was wrong, what he did to you. I'm not denying that." And neither was Kirby. He knew, better than anyone, how terribly he'd hurt Matt.

"I was taught to tell people that my daddy was a cowboy drifter and that my mom never even knew his real name." A sharp laugh rattled from his throat. "Even now, if someone asks about my father, I still recount that same fake story."

"Does your mother's husband know the truth?"

"She couldn't bear to keep lying to him, so she told him right before they got married. Of course, it's only been a few months, so they're still in the honeymoon stages. But he would never betray her trust. Or mine. He stays out of our personal business."

"What about your ex?" Libby thought about his marriage and how quickly it had ended. "Did you ever tell her?"

"No."

"Did you ever want to tell her?"

"No."

"Why not?"

"Because being Kirby's son doesn't matter to me, and I didn't want it to matter to her, either. Besides, we had other things to contend with." He searched Libby's gaze, as if he were searching for someone's grave. "Did you know that she was a widow? Like you?"

"It came up in my research." But Libby hadn't expected him to make a comparison in such a disturbing way. "According to what I uncovered, her name is Sandra Molloy, and she and her first husband had two kids and owned the dry cleaner's in town." It wasn't much to go on, but it was the only information she had.

"She went by Sandy, and she sold that business when she married me. She cried about her husband nearly every day. Do you still think about your husband?"

"Of course I do." Libby glanced away, wishing that Matt would stop staring at her. "But I've come to terms with my grief." With the tears and pain, with waking up alone. "I'm not letting it rule my life."

"Then why can I see him, like a ghost inside you?"

"You don't even know what he looks like."

"I didn't mean it literally."

She thought about the images of Becker on her phone. The happy, smiling, easygoing father of her child. He was so different from Matt. "You're just seeing what you want to see."

"Why would I want to see something like that when I look at you? When I'm this close—" he created a tiny space between his thumb and forefinger "—to giving up the fight and kissing you?"

"Then do it, damn you. Just do it." She didn't want to keep fantasizing about being kissed by him. She just wanted to lose herself in the feeling, no matter how wrong it was.

He leaned into her, his gaze challenging hers. Was he baiting her stop him, to push him away?

Libby challenged him right back, staring him down, daring him to go through with it.

Heaven help them.

He kept coming toward her, until his hands were tangled in her hair and his mouth was fused passionately to hers.

Just the way she'd imagined it.

Three

Matt cursed in his mind. He was getting consumed with this woman in ways that were driving him mad.

He undid his seat belt and so did she. The straps were too confining, and they both needed to be free.

With his eyes tightly closed, he deepened the kiss, craving the taste of her. He pushed his tongue into her mouth. She reacted just as uncontrollably, pressing closer to him, her hunger equal to his.

Hellfire, he thought. He was getting hard beneath his jeans. From a kiss. From one soft, slick, wet…

She wrapped her arms around his neck, and he pulled her, like a rag doll, right over the center console and onto his lap.

He envisioned how they must look, parked on the

road that overlooked his old place, with her straddling him in the driver's seat, the steering wheel butting against her back.

Matt felt like a teenager, making out in the middle of the day, his hormones jerking and jumping.

He wound his hands more fully in her hair. He liked how wild and wavy it was. She rocked forward, rubbing him where it hurt, where it felt good, where his zipper made friction with hers.

They kept kissing, mindless and carnal. She mewled, then moaned, hot and sweet, and he suspected that she would make those same fevered sounds if he was deep inside her.

When they came up for air, she asked, "Is the truck still running? Is that the vibration I feel?"

"I think it's us." He'd shut the engine off earlier. Hadn't he? Just to be sure, he double-checked. "It's not running."

"It's not? Are you sure?"

"I'm positive. But we should stop now."

"You first."

"You want me to end it?" He didn't appreciate her leaving it up to him. "You're the one who's sitting on my lap."

"And you're the one who put me there."

Touché, he thought. "Yeah, but you can climb off me and get back in your own seat." His frustration was building, at himself, at her. He wanted to strip her naked, right here, right now.

"I could." Her eyes were glazed over and her hair

was totally mussed, maybe even knotted in spots. Her frustration was mounting, too. "Or you could make me."

"Screw that." He kissed her again, harder this time, making good on his threat to bite her.

"Ouch." She flinched, then kissed him right back.

A heartbeat later, he said, "It was only a nibble."

"Says you. My lips are going to be swollen."

"They already are." And she wore it insanely well. "Now get off me before I do something I'll regret."

"You're already regretting this, and so am I."

"So go back on your own side of the truck."

She didn't budge. She stayed there, desire bristling from her pores. She snared his gaze, her eyelashes long and fluttery. "You owe me a cookie."

Seriously? She was going to hold him to that? "Fine. As soon as I can take the wheel, we'll go to the bakery."

"I want coffee, too." She crawled over the console and nearly kneed him in the nuts, missing him by mere inches. But she didn't even notice that she'd almost done it.

Matt snarled to himself. He deserved a swift kick, but the entire situation still made him angry. Everything about it ticked him off. Especially what he couldn't have—like Libby sprawled out beneath him.

He wanted to take her home and make hot-blooded love to her, to be rough and animalistic, to bite her again a hundred more times.

She settled onto her seat, lowered the visor and

gawked at herself in the mirror. "Oh, my goodness. What did you do to my hair? I look like a blowfish."

Since when did fish have hair? Spiny things coming out of their heads, maybe. "You liked it when I was doing it."

She finger-combed her way through the mess. "We're never kissing again. Not ever."

"I know." He tugged at his jeans, trying to make his bulge less noticeable. "It was awful of us." Awfully hot, awfully barbaric, awfully amazing. He could think of a hundred mixed-up ways to describe what they'd done.

She kept fussing with her hair, struggling to tame it.

"You're making it worse," he said.

"What?" she asked. "Your hard-on or my hair?"

"Your hair, smarty."

She glanced at his lap. "Not from where I'm sitting."

"Don't start." But it was too late. They both burst into a quick, crazy laugh. The situation was too disturbing to keep it bottled up.

She raised the visor, giving up on her hair. He gave up on adjusting his jeans, too. Then he went serious and asked, "Are you going to tell Kirby that we kissed?"

"I would never do that. This was a private moment between you and me. It's no one else's business."

"So what happens between you and me is private, but the rest of my life isn't?"

"Your relationship with Kirby is the only part of your life that I'll be writing about." She glanced down at the canyon house. "Yours and your mother's. And that's why it's so important for me to get your input, and hers, too. I have lots of interview questions, for both of you."

"No doubt you do. But I'm not signing a release or answering them. If I tell you anything, it's going to be the way we've been doing it, off the record." He followed her line of sight to the house. He remembered his mom crying on the night Kirby had ended their affair. How she'd sat outside and bawled in the moonlight. Matt had been old enough then to understand what was going on. He'd sensed it was over for him, too, that his dad's sporadic visits would become even less frequent. He'd even worried that Kirby would eventually stop coming around at all. And he'd been right on both counts. So painfully right.

"Please, just think about it," Libby implored him.

He blew out a breath. "I can't willingly be part of your book." He didn't want to bleed all over the pages of his old man's self-serving biography. "I just can't do it."

"If you were involved in the book, I would get to know you, better than I am now."

He laughed, as foolishly as before. "You're getting to know me just fine."

"That's not funny." She rolled her big blue eyes, frowned, smiled, shook her messy-haired head. "Well, maybe it is."

He noticed that her lips were still sexily swollen. "Buckle up." He reached over and pulled the strap across her body, doing it for her. "I've got to back out of here."

And try to forget that he'd ever kissed her.

Libby couldn't believe that she'd taunted Matt to kiss her. That she wouldn't get off his lap. That she let it go that far.

She needed to be flogged, tortured for her idiotic behavior. What part of professionalism had escaped her? She'd been acting up since the moment she'd met him, being so coy and cute, pushing her attraction to him in directions it wasn't supposed to go.

When they arrived at the bakery, he parked directly in front of the small, pastel-colored building. The town itself was quaint, with its Main Street simplicity and homespun vibe.

"Maybe I should order a tart," she said.

"Those fruit-filled things?"

"Yes, but that was a joke." She pointed to herself. "A *tart*, get it?"

He didn't laugh. "Don't call yourself names, Libby. I'm just as responsible as you are. We're just lucky that we stopped when we did."

"It wasn't luck. It was restraint."

"You know what I mean."

She most certainly did. She'd never kissed anyone that ferociously before, not even Becker.

They got out of the truck, and she glanced at the bakery window. A big, frothy, three-tiered wedding cake was showcased. The bride and groom on top looked a bit like her and Matt. It was their coloring, the bride being blonde and the groom having black hair. She doubted that Matt noticed the cake, let alone the topper. He headed straight for the front door.

"Let's go get those cookies," he said.

She nodded, and they went inside. A middle-aged woman in blue jeans and a crisp white apron greeted them. She smiled and acknowledged Matt by name. The bakery lady knew him? This piqued Libby's curiosity.

But soon she discovered that he'd gone to high school with the woman's son. In a town this size, Libby shouldn't have been surprised. Most of the locals probably knew each other. It did make her wonder about Matt's experiences in high school and if he was as much a loner then as he seemed to be now.

He chose the cookies randomly, four dozen of them, in every shape, size and color they had.

"What are we supposed to do with all of those?" Libby asked as they left the bakery and set out on foot, heading for the little coffee joint across the street.

"You can take them back to your cabin later."

"Chance would love them if he were here."

He stopped midstride. "Chance?"

"Chance Mitchell Penn. My son." She watched the troubled emotion that crossed Matt's face. She hadn't meant to blurt out Chance's name, but at least she'd gone ahead and said it.

"You named him after Kirby's song?"

"Initially, it was Becker's idea. But I thought it

was a brilliant choice." She was going to stand by her child's name, no matter how uncomfortable it made Matt. "If we had a girl, we were going to call her Lilly Fay, after the saloon girl in the song. The one Chance Mitchell loves and leaves."

"I don't like any of Kirby's songs, least of all that one. It came out when..."

"When what?" she asked. They stood on the side-walk, with Matt clutching the pink bakery box.

"When I fell off the roof of our house and broke my arm. It was just after my ninth birthday, and I was pre-tending to be Chance Mitchell. I was crawling around up there with a toy gun, a six-shooter, strapped to my hip. I was hiding from the law."

Libby reached up and skimmed his jaw. She knew she shouldn't be touching him, but she wanted to com-fort him somehow. "You must have liked the song then, or else why would you be pretending to be Chance?"

He took a step back, forcing her to lower her hand. "Sure. I liked his music when I was a kid. But it started to grate on me later."

She tried to draw more of the story out of him. "Did they put your broken arm in a cast?"

He nodded. "Kirby never saw it, though. He was on his *Outlaw at Large* tour, promoting the Chance Mitchell album, and my arm healed before he stopped back to see us."

"I'm sorry he didn't make more time for you then."

"I don't care anymore."

That was a lie, she thought. He cared far too much.

"Kirby told me that he was impressed with your junior rodeo accomplishments. That you were just a little tyke, riding and roping like the devil was inside you."

"What does he know about it? He never attended any of my events. All he saw were the videos Mom showed him."

"He remembers those videos. He thinks about them when he's feeling guilty and blue. He wrote a song about you, too, but he hasn't recorded it yet."

"Holy crap." Matt tightened his grip on the box. "That's all I need, to be immortalized in one of his frigging songs."

"He's not going to record it until the two of you become father and son."

"Then he's never going to put it out there." Matt approached the crosswalk and stepped off the curb.

She followed him. "The song is called 'The Boy I Left Behind.' He played it for me. It's beautiful, raw and touching."

"That's a low blow."

"What is? Me telling you how good it is?"

"No. Him playing it for you. He's using you, Libby. He's pushing you around like a pawn."

"He's sharing his life with me. That's my role in all of this, to document his life, to write about his feelings." After they made it to the other side of the street, she said, "I know you don't believe that he ever loved you, but in his own tortured way, he did. You were the part of himself that he couldn't control. He promised his wife that he would never father a child from any of his affairs, and then you came along. The baby that wasn't supposed to exist. His secret. A sweet little boy who needed more than his daddy knew how to give."

"I'm well aware of what he promised his wife. It's the reason I had to stay in the shadows, the excuse that was drilled into my head. My famous father had another family, and it would hurt them if they knew about me. But his wife found out and divorced him, anyway."

"She's over it now. She and Kirby are friends again. I haven't met her yet, but I'll be interviewing her for the book." Her name was Melinda, and she was a former fashion model who used her celebrity to create a cosmetics and skin care line. Her face, her brand, were featured in TV infomercials. "She agrees with Kirby that everything should be out in the open now."

"Of course she does. He always gets women to forgive him. And can we please talk about something else? I'm sick of my dad."

"Okay. We'll work on other topics." She sent him her best smile, even if he was still scowling, much too fiercely, at her.

Matt and Libby sat outside at a café table. He drank his coffee black. She put sugar *and* an artificial sweetener in hers, along with cream and milk. He'd never seen anyone mix so much stuff together in one cup.

She opened the cookies. "Look how cute they are." She lifted a smiley face from the bunch. "This one looks like me."

He took it from her and held it upside down. "And now it looks like me."

Her eyes twinkled. "At least you have a sense of humor about that disposition of yours." She removed a flower-shaped cookie from the box and nibbled on it, leaving the happy face for him.

He broke off a piece of its smile. "I'm sorry if I've been such lousy company since you met me. I'm not always this difficult to get along with."

She ate more of the flower, dropping crumbs onto the table. "I expected you to react to me with resistance. I just didn't expect for us to..."

Fall into lust with each other? "We already agreed to put that to rest, so there's no point in rehashing it."

"You're right. I shouldn't have brought it up."

Yeah, he thought, but were they fooling themselves in believing that they would never do it again? Even now, as she made a pretty little mess out of her cookie, he was fixated on her mouth. Forgetting that he'd kissed her was proving to be impossible.

"Where did you get married?" she asked suddenly. "Was it on your ranch?"

The hits just kept on coming with this girl. Sucker punches to the gut. "Why are you asking me about my wedding?"

"Because I'm curious about you, and the couple on top on the wedding cake at the bakery sort of looked like us."

"I didn't see a cake like that."

"You weren't paying attention." She gestured to the other side of the street. "It's in the window."

He didn't turn to look, not from this distance. "If I tell you about my wedding, then you have to tell me about yours, too." He wasn't going to stab himself in the heart without making her do the same. "Turnabout is fair play, or however that saying goes."

"All right. But I asked you first."

"Then no, I didn't get married on the ranch."

"Why not?" She gazed at him from across the table. "It seems like the perfect place for it."

"Sandy didn't want to get married in this area. She wanted to go away, to elope. So she left her kids with her parents and we flew to Las Vegas. She didn't tell her folks or anyone else what we were doing until we got back. I kept quiet, too." He'd respected Sandy's wishes. "She wanted it to be different from her first wedding. No prepping or planning, no guests, no fuss, no muss, no hoopla."

Libby angled her head. "Did any of that matter to you?"

"Not really. I just wanted to have a family—her and the kids. But I should have sensed that she was trying too hard to make it different from her first wedding, with us going to Vegas and whatnot."

Her eyes grew wider. "You didn't get married by an Elvis impersonator, did you?"

He stifled a laugh. Trust Libby to say something funny. "It was just a normal minister in a quiet little chapel. They provided the witnesses, but none of them looked like Elvis, either."

"Did you get a honeymoon suite at your hotel?"

"No. We just stayed in a regular room."

"Was that Sandy's idea, too?"

He nodded. "She didn't want the hotel making a fuss over us. At the time, it seemed okay. But if I ever got married again, I would have the wedding right here in my hometown and make it a celebratory occasion."

She removed another cookie—a frosted cowboy boot—from the box. "So you're planning on having another wife?"

"Someday, maybe. But she's not going to be someone who's hurting over another man. I'm never going to put myself through that again." He leaned back in his chair, playing it cool, hating how exposed he felt. "So I guess that leaves you out, huh?"

She wagged the boot at him. "Is that supposed to be a joke? I told you I was doing fine in that regard."

He didn't believe her bravado. He was certain that she cried when no one was there to see her do it. "You have to admit that we would make a terrible match." Great kisses. Horrendous fights. "We don't get along worth a lick."

"True." She flicked a crumb at him. "But it's your pissy personality that would be the problem."

"Right. Because you're such a gem." He came forward in his seat. "So what's the deal with your wedding? You owe me the details."

"First off, I was pregnant when I got married." She

pulled her blouse out in front of her, stretching the fabric. "Almost seven months."

"Oh, my." He exaggerated his drawl. "Do tell."

"Don't mock me. I was a lovely bride."

"I'm sure you were." He pictured her glowing like a pregnant lady should. "But why did you wait so long to seal the deal?"

"We couldn't decide if we should get married before or after the baby was born. We thought it would be cute to wait until he or she could be part of the ceremony. But our families convinced us to do it before."

"I agree. I think it's better for kids to have married parents." Matt sure as hell wished that he'd come into this world legitimately. "When did you know you were having a boy?"

"On the day Chance was born. We could have found out sooner, but we wanted to be surprised. That's part of the beauty of having children. To let them surprise you."

He drank his coffee. "I bet you wore a sparkly dress."

She toyed with the rim of her cup. "At the wedding? Yes, it was quite glittery. We got married on the beach, in our cowboy boots. Mine were white and decorated with rhinestones." She gazed at her half-eaten cookie. "I still have them."

And her dress, too, no doubt, preserved for all time. Sandy had kept her first gown. Matt didn't have a clue what happened to the dress she'd worn when she'd married him. "That doesn't sound like a typical beach wedding."

"It wasn't. We created a country theme. We put up a rustic wooden arch decorated with horseshoes and flowers, and I walked down the aisle to 'Chantilly Heart.'"

Well, of course she did, he thought. That was right up her alley. "I should have known that you would pick one of Kirby's songs."

"It's such a gorgeous ballad. It's a favorite at Western-themed weddings."

Matt turned droll. "I'd rather have an Elvis impersonator." He would've welcomed a guy in a white jumpsuit over a Kirby Talbot tune any day. It was beyond him how his dad could write such compelling love songs, when you took into account what a womanizer he was. "Maybe I'll do the Elvis thing next time."

Her laughter rang rich and true. "I really like you, Matt, even if we don't get along worth a lick."

A lick of sugar, he thought, as she polished off the cowboy boot cookie. "I begrudgingly liked you from the start."

"Glad to hear it. Well, not the begrudgingly part." She quickly asked, "Will you take me to see your old high school?"

There she went again, throwing him off-kilter. "What for?"

"I got curious after the bakery lady mentioned it."

"It's just a typical small-town high school." He

didn't see the point in dredging up yet another aspect of his youth. "It's nothing special."

"I'd still like to see it."

"It's a Sunday in July. It'll be closed."

"Is it fenced, locked and gated?"

"No. They don't have those types of security issues around here."

"Then why can't we walk around the grounds?"

He shook his head. "You sure are pesky."

"I already warned you that I was. Don't you remember? The most persuasive cowgirl you'll ever meet."

He corrected her. "Yeah, and besides the fact that I told you you're not a cowgirl, *pesky* and *persuasive* don't mean the same thing."

She dusted the sprinkles from her fingertips. "In my case they do. So, what were you like in school?"

He shrugged. "I wasn't one of the popular kids, but I wasn't a social outcast, either. Believe it or not, I had friends." He still did, even if he rarely saw them anymore. His closest buddies were happily married, making him feel even more miserably divorced.

Libby asked, "What about the secret you were keeping about who your father was? Didn't that bother you when you were in high school?"

"By then, I was used to the lie, and Kirby wasn't coming around anymore, anyway. The toughest part, I guess, was that I was the only Native American kid at my school. This town doesn't have much of a Native population." He finished his coffee, pushed his cup aside. "I'm registered with the Cherokee Nation, but I also have a teeny bit of Tonkawa blood. I'm not an enrolled member of the Tonkawa tribe. But I heard they were originally from this area, and they claimed to have descended from a mystical wolf."

Libby stared at him. "Like the wolf Kirby said you were? You and your gold eyes?"

"Not all wolves' eyes are yellow. Some are brown or gray or green. I read somewhere that cubs are born with blue eyes, but they fade within six to ten weeks, changing into the adult color."

"Were you born with blue eyes?"

"No." His were always this shade. "Yours are certainly blue." They were especially bright in the sunlight.

"Could it be that I'm part wolf, too, but mine never changed?"

"Nope." He came up with an animal identity that suited her far better. "You're part badger, that's what you are."

"Oh, that's a good one." She grinned, dimples and all. "And badger that I am, I still want to see your high school. I'm not letting up about that."

"All right. That'll be our next stop." Another trip down memory lane. Call him crazy. But he wanted to spend more time with her, even if he had to give up bits and pieces of himself to do it.

Four

As Matt and Libby walked around Creek Hill High, he felt like a warped tour guide. He wasn't an outcast in school, but the shell he'd built around himself when he was a kid was still there. He was certain that Libby had built a shell around herself, too. Maybe not when she was a child, but later, after her husband died. He didn't believe for a city slicker minute that she was handling her loss as well as she claimed to be.

"I told you this place was nothing special," he said. They continued to stroll along the grass-flanked pathways.

"I think it's nice, cozy." She glanced around. "It's definitely a lot smaller than the school I attended. I was the editor of our newspaper. I worked on the yearbook, too. We had a journalism club. That's where I spent most of my time."

"I should have guessed as much. The little writer." He looked into those blue eyes of hers. "Did you listen to country music and wear Western clothes back then?" He wanted to get a complete picture of her. He was just as curious about her youth as she was about his.

"Yes, I was into it then. But it wasn't just the clothes and the music that fascinated me. I used to watch rodeos on TV, and I would get these dreamy, sexy crushes on the cowboys. Sort of like I have on you." She winced. "Sorry. I shouldn't have said that."

His body reacted, his pulse galloping from his head to his toes. "At least now I know why you kissed me the way you did."

"Right. My latent cowboy fantasies." She swept her hand through the air, as if she were trying to wave those fantasies away. "I got interested in horses, too, and asked my parents if I could take riding lessons, so they took me to the local equestrian center. I wanted my own horse, but we couldn't afford it. My parents are just working folk. Mom was a supermarket checker, and Dad sells cars. She's retired now and has a small pension. He still works for a dealer. They've been married for thirty-five years. They wanted more kids, but Mom kept losing babies. I was the only one she carried full-term."

"I'll bet they're wonderful grandparents." He imagined them doting on Libby's son.

"They're the best. They adore Chance. So do Becker's parents. I'm still really close to them, too. Becker was from a big family, brothers and sisters and aunts and uncles and cousins. Chance loves hanging out with all of them."

Matt escorted her to the back of the campus, where the football field was. "Where did you meet Becker?"

She made a beeline for the bleachers. But it took her a moment to say, "It was at one of your dad's concerts. I sat next to him at the show. I was with some friends from the equestrian center, and he was with two of his brothers."

Matt frowned. Of all the places she could've met her husband, did it have to be connected to Kirby? "How old were you?"

"Nineteen, and Becker was twenty. He wasn't the type I dreamed about. He wasn't a cowboy or a rough-and-tumble guy. It was his heart I saw, his openness, his kindness. But he shared my love of country, and that mattered, too, of course." She climbed onto the first set of bleachers. "He was my first. Not my first boyfriend, but the first man I…"

"Slept with?" Matt stepped up onto the bleachers, too.

She nodded. "It was gentle and romantic, the way it should be for a girl's first time. But it was always like that when we were together."

An immediate urge to apologize came over him. "I didn't mean to hurt you when we kissed, Libby."

She blinked, teetered on her feet. They had yet to sit

down. "You didn't hurt me. It felt good." She sucked her bottom lip between her teeth. "A good kind of pain."

He knew precisely what she meant. "I'm not normally that aggressive."

"I just bring it out in you?"

"So it seems." And if he had it to do over, he would probably behave just as roughly. But he would try to be romantic somehow, too.

She finally sat, and so did he. Silent, they stared out at the empty field. He was tempted to hold her hand, like a high school boy might do, but he kept his calloused paws to himself. They weren't teenagers, and he wasn't dating her.

"When did you quit competing in junior rodeos?" she asked.

He turned to look at her. Her hair was still messy from earlier, tangled beautifully around her face. "When I was thirteen."

"The year after Kirby ended his relationship with your mom? Is that significant as to why you quit?"

"Overall, it was a challenging time in my life, with me being a teenager, and their breakup only made it more difficult. I didn't understand why Mom was still defending Kirby, especially since they weren't together anymore. I was starting to hate him, to hold him accountable for his actions, but she was asking me to be patient, saying that he was going through a bad time and needed help."

"With what? The drinking? The drugs?"

Matt nodded. "He was partying really heavily then. By that time I hardly ever saw him. Not that he was a constant in my life, anyway. But he was coming by even less and less, and on the rare occasions that he did show up, he was either high or hungover." Soon after that, Kirby stopped visiting him at all.

"I'm so sorry that he put you through that. Even your brothers mentioned how difficult his addictions were for them to tolerate. But he's completely clean and sober now."

"Did they help him with his recovery? Were they part of it?"

"Yes, they were."

A stream of anger, of envy, of everything being the odd kid out had made him feel, shot through his veins. He hadn't been allowed to help, even if he'd wanted to. Which he didn't, he told himself. Kirby didn't deserve his empathy. "What about Tommy and that supposedly wild streak of his?"

"Tommy doesn't drink or do drugs. Most of his wildness is in the form of his music, his rebellious lyrics and his antics on stage. The reckless stunts he pulls. He takes risks that he shouldn't, climbing up riggings and swinging from ropes that weren't designed to hold him, jumping off platforms without warning. He drives his road crew crazy with worry."

Matt scoffed. Tommy sounded like an idiot to him.

Libby continued, "Kirby says that Tommy has always been a daredevil, even when he was a kid. I heard that Tommy is supposed to be wild in bed, too.

Or that's the reputation he has, with lots of groupies hanging around."

Matt didn't give two figs about Tommy's conquests. But he cared about how it affected Libby. "Are you attracted to him?"

"Who? Tommy?" She shook her head. "I haven't been attracted to anyone since Becker passed." She paused, bit her lip, then said, "Except for you."

Matt wanted to kiss her again. He wanted it so badly, he ached from the need. "I wish you weren't writing my dad's book." He hated how closely tied she was to his father and Tommy and the rest of the Talbots.

"I would have never even met you if I wasn't."

The urge to kiss her got stronger, more painful. But he kept his distance. "Maybe it would be better if we'd never met."

"We can't go back in time and erase it."

"I'm never going to sign a release or let you interview me."

"I think eventually you will. You need to get Kirby off your chest. Look at all of the things you've told me so far."

"But you can't use any of it in the book, so it doesn't matter what I say or how much I reveal. I could tell you every agonizing thing that's in my heart and you still couldn't write about it."

"Are you going to do that, Matt?"

"Do what?"

"Tell me every agonizing thing in your heart?"

"I might. If you tell me what's in yours."

"I don't have as much to tell as you do."

He called her bluff. "You're twenty-nine with a six-year-old son and a husband who died. You've got plenty of agony."

She sighed. "I'm not Sandy. You can't keep looking at me as if I'm her."

"I see what I see. A woman who lost her mate."

"Yes, but everyone mourns differently. And I already told you that I've accepted being a widow. I have a support group in my family and in Becker's. I got professional counseling, too, and that was a big step for me. It helped me understand the stages of grief and move toward a place of hope."

"And yet three years later you're at my ranch, having mixed-up feelings for me. The ex-husband of another widow. That's got to mean something, Libby."

She shook her head. "I'm not getting attached to you because you had a wife whose husband died. That's not why you make me feel the way you do."

"Not consciously, maybe. But it has to be part of it. You knew I was married to a widow when you met me. You researched my background."

"That wasn't the reason I felt something for you when I first met you. It was just our chemistry. The instant heat." She glanced away, as if she were feeling it now. Or fighting it. Or whatever it was she was doing.

He said, "In the beginning what Sandy felt for me was sexual, too, all tied up with her grief."

Libby returned her gaze to his. "That still doesn't

give you the right to say that my attraction to you is associated with grief."

Based on his experiences, he believed otherwise. But for now, he went quiet, waiting for her to resume their dialogue.

A moment later, she asked, "How did you and Sandy meet?"

"She was at the bar with some of her girlfriends, drinking a little, playing songs on the jukebox. I'd seen Sandy and her husband around town before, but I'd never officially met either of them. Sandy is older than me by about six years, and so was he." Matt gestured to their surroundings. "They both went to school here, just not at the same time as I did."

"But you still knew who Sandy was when you saw her at the bar?"

"Yes. I also knew that she'd lost her husband. That he passed away a year or so before. His name was Greg Molloy." But maybe Libby knew that already? Maybe his name had come up in her research? Matt couldn't tell by her reaction.

Either way, she went silent for a second. Then she asked, "What happened to him? How did he die?"

Matt relayed the details, tragic as they were. "He was in a plane crash. An out-of-town relative of his owned one of those little two-seater aircrafts, and there was a malfunction that sent them spinning to the ground."

"How awful." Libby pressed both hands to her

chest. "Just the way you described it makes me hurt for Sandy."

"It gave her nightmares." Matt couldn't begin to count the number of times she'd awakened next to him, crying out from a bad dream. "But she still managed to get on a plane afterward. Or commercial flights, anyway." Like the one that had taken them to Vegas to be married. But maybe that was a bit of a death wish on her part—the flight, the wedding, the whole damned thing.

"So tell me more about how you met. And what happened at the bar."

"I was waiting for a buddy of mine, but he called and said he couldn't make it. I stayed there by myself, watching everyone in the place and giving myself something to do. I've never been much of a barfly, even if I still go there now and then." To escape, he thought, to be alone in a crowd. "I noticed Sandy and her friends. There was a guy who kept bothering Sandy, who was getting too rowdy, and she kept trying to push him away. So I stepped in and took over, telling him to beat it. After that, I hung out with Sandy and her girlfriends. It was their idea to take her out to begin with. She hadn't gone anywhere since Greg died." The more memories he conjured up, the more vivid they became. "As the evening wore on, her friends wanted to leave and Sandy wanted to stay there with me. So I promised her friends that I would get her home safely."

"And they were okay with that?"

"They trusted me, so it wasn't an issue. I'd actually met some of them before, and they knew I owned the Flying Creek Ranch and had a decent reputation. I doubt they would have left her alone with me if they thought I was going to sleep with her that night. But that wasn't my intention." He preferred to date the usual way, getting to know someone first. "I never even kissed her at the bar."

"When did you kiss her?" Libby quietly asked.

"At her front door, after I drove her home. And that's how I was going to leave it, with a chaste kiss. I figured I would get her phone number and we would go from there. But it got hot and heavy. Only I didn't start it, the way I did with you in the truck. She initiated the sexual stuff." His memories went raw. "It didn't dawn on me that she was transposing her loneliness into lust." He hadn't expected to fall in love with her, either, or to marry her later, or to try to heal her broken heart. None of that had crossed his mind on that fateful night. "She cried about Greg afterward. Deep, soul-wrenching tears. So I held her until morning. I whispered in her ear, I stroked my hand down her hair, I told her everything would be all right."

"That was wonderful of you to console her, Matt, even if sleeping with her so soon wasn't a good idea."

Even now, with as messed up as everything was, he wanted to touch Libby, to skim her cheek, to feel her skin beneath his fingertips. He couldn't seem to get this woman out of his blood. "If you and I had gone too far today—"

She shook her head. "We shouldn't even be talking about this. We're not going to be together like that."

"You're right. We're not." But he still wasn't convinced that they weren't headed for trouble. As overpowering as their chemistry was, anything could happen.

Libby stood in front of the mirror, her hair damp from the shower and a towel wrapped snugly around her body. She couldn't stop thinking about the things Matt had said to her yesterday.

He was wrong about her. Her attraction to him didn't put her in the same category as his former wife. Libby wasn't following in Sandy's shaky footsteps. She wasn't getting close to Matt to fill a void being widowed had left behind.

As much as Libby missed Becker, she wasn't trapped in the same kind of grief as Sandy's. If by some crazy, hungry, uncontrollable chance she decided to make love with Matt, she wouldn't break down in his arms. She would simply appreciate Matt for who he was.

Her living, breathing fantasy.

She dropped her towel and gazed at herself in the mirror. She was young and single, free and alone. So maybe she should just cave into those urges and sleep with Matt.

She squeezed her eyes shut, warning herself to back off. She was here to do a job, to gather research, to convince Matt to be interviewed. Having an affair with him wasn't part of the deal.

Opening her eyes, she picked up her towel and hung it back on the rack. She planned on going to the lodge for breakfast. After that, she wasn't sure what she was going to do. She intended to see Matt, of course. The more time she spent with him, the more likely she was to convince him to be part of the book. Because, really, that was all that mattered.

Right? *Right.*

Libby scrunched her hair, working a hair-polishing serum through it to make it shine. She put on her makeup, adding a dollop of gloss to her lips, making them shine, too. Next, she got dressed, shrugging into skinny jeans. The blouse she chose left her midriff bare.

She rummaged through her jewelry and accessorized her outfit with silver hoop earrings and a rhinestone-studded skull-and-crossbones pendant. She yanked on a pair of tall black cowboy boots, tucking her skin-tight jeans into them. Finally, she plopped a black Stetson on her head.

It certainly wasn't her typical morning attire. "But what the heck?" she said aloud. At least she wasn't cowering from her libido. She needed to look rebellious, to feel sexy, even if she wasn't going to act on her feelings.

She returned to her makeup case and dug around for her liquid eyeliner. With precision, she created cat eyes, making them dark and bold. Last, she spritzed a spicy perfume into the air and walked through the mist, letting it settle around her. Now she was ready, totally ready, to present herself as the strong and steady widow that she was.

She poked her head out the door to see if Matt's truck was in his driveway. Sure enough, it was.

With her chin held high and her boot heels kicking up dirt, she strode over to his cabin and rapped on the door.

He answered her summons, his gaze roaming the length of her. "Damn, Libby. What poor sap did you just consume for breakfast?"

Was that his way of saying that she looked like a man-eater? "Breakfast is precisely why I'm here. I was hoping you'd join me at the lodge. They put on a darned fine spread, in case you haven't heard."

He was still eyeballing her. "Come to think of it, I have heard. But I already had a bowl of cereal."

She poked at the flatness of his stomach. He was wearing a plain gray T-shirt tucked into his jeans. "Surely you have room in there for eggs and potatoes. Or gravy and biscuits. Mmm," she said for effect. "That's my favorite."

He glanced at her pendant, then shifted his attention to her feline-inspired eye makeup. "I think you need a guy with a big flashy motorcycle to take you."

She fingered the skull. She liked that he was being glib. She was in that kind of mood, too. "I'd rather have a guy with a big, flashy stallion." She batted her lashes. She had on two coats of mascara today. "Oh, wait. You have one of those, don't you?"

"Indeed I do." He played along with her. "But I

think you'd be safer in my truck. The stallion would probably get one whiff of you and fall head over heels."

"Promising Spirit." She remembered seeing the horse's name in the ranch brochure. She'd also gotten a gander at his picture, and he was quite the buckskin beauty. "I'll take my chances." Suddenly she was no longer flirting. She was just being her regular self again. "Do you have any new foals?"

Matt went back to normal, too. "We've got three on the way. One of them should arrive in about ten days or so."

"Just around the time Chance is coming." Her son would be here by then, along with Libby's mother.

"I'd be glad to show him the foal when it's born."

"That would be great." She suspected that Matt had been a good caregiver to Sandy's children. "He's going to love your ranch. He's going to be enthralled with you, too. The man in charge."

"I like kids." He ducked his head and stepped away from the door. "Come in and I'll get my boots on."

She entered his home. It appeared to be professionally decorated, similar to her accommodations, with rough-hewn furnishings and Old West artifacts on the walls. But she didn't catch sight of anything that defined him in a personal way, no photographs or items that spoke his name. This could have been just another rental cabin. "So you're going to accompany me to breakfast?"

"I might as well. But I have to work afterward." He paused, as if he were debating something. He finally said, "There's a hayride and marshmallow roast tonight." Another long, drawn-out pause, then, "We can get together later for that, if you want to."

"Thanks. That sounds fun." She appreciated the invitation, even as hesitantly as he'd extended it.

She watched him walk to the master bedroom to get his boots. The door was open, a portion of his bed visible. His covers were turned down and rumpled from where he'd slept.

He returned with his socks and boots and sat on the sofa to put them on. She perched on the edge of a leather chair, but she could still see the corner of his unmade bed.

Blocking it out of her mind, she asked, "Did Sandy and the kids live here with you?" She'd been wondering about that, and now she had the opportunity to find out.

He looked up from his task. "I have a house on the other side of the ranch."

"You do? I thought maybe you were going to build a house for you and Sandy and the kids, but things ended before you got the chance to do it."

"It was my house before I got married, before Sandy came into my life. I built it at the same time as the ranch. I just haven't felt like living there since the divorce, so I moved into this cabin." He angled his head. "And how is it that we're back to talking about my ex?"

"I'm not going to avoid the subject just because you compared me to her." She refused to fall prey to that.

"I already told you that I'm not Sandy, and it isn't right for you to lump us together."

"Yes, you told me. But what are we doing, Libby?"

Her response was quick. "We're going to breakfast."

He furrowed his brow. "That's not what I meant."

She knew what he meant: What were they doing, steeped in uncomfortable feelings for each other? But that was a question she couldn't quite answer. "I'm just trying to convince you to participate in Kirby's book."

"Showing up at my door in that getup? You look like you're going to ride me hard and fast and put me away wet."

Her mouth went dry. Suddenly she was thirsty as sin, in more ways than one. But she didn't hide the truth. She said, "I considered it."

He stared at her, and she noticed how he hadn't yet pulled one of his pant legs down to his boot.

"You did?" he asked. "When?"

"This morning, after my shower, I contemplated having an affair with you."

He rolled his pant leg down. "And?"

"And I reminded myself that it wouldn't be right. That I didn't come to your ranch to sleep with you. But that doesn't mean I'm going to stop fantasizing about it." Hot and dizzy, she headed for his kitchen. "Is it okay if I get a glass of water?"

He was still staring at her. "Help yourself."

Help herself to what? Anything she wanted, or just the water? She went for the H2O. She located a plastic tumbler and poured a drink from the tap.

Once she was steadier on her feet, she said, "We better go before everyone else beats us to the buffet."

"That's a good idea." He didn't return to the topic of their nonexistent affair. He didn't say another word about it.

They went to breakfast, both of them behaving, at least outwardly, as though it had never been mentioned at all.

Five

Matt and Libby rode in the back of a straw-filled, horse-drawn wagon that they had all to themselves, not counting the driver. The shiny red cart had high rails for a certain amount of privacy, with plenty of comfort for two.

The rest of the people were ahead of them in big noisy groups, making Matt and Libby's the last wagon trailing quietly behind. But he preferred it that way. On this moonlit evening, his mind was elsewhere. He was still trying to absorb the sexy little things Libby had told him earlier.

"It's beautiful out here," she said. "All the twinkling lights and night-blooming flowers." She peered over the side. "Oh, and look at the colorful bottles hanging from the trees."

Matt merely nodded. He'd seen all of this a zillion times before. He'd even decorated some of it himself.

At this point, he just wanted to get Libby out of his system. To make long, hard love to her. To fulfill their mutual screwed-up fantasies, no matter what the consequences. But he knew better than to act on impulse. Apparently Libby knew better, too. What a responsible pair they were, he thought. Torturing themselves.

"What's the significance of the bottles?" she asked.

He frowned. "I'm sorry. What?"

"The bottles. What's the purpose of hanging them like that?"

He snapped into owner-of-the-ranch mode, doing his best to be her hayride host. "Mostly they're just garden ornaments. Or that's what they've become in this day and age. A bit of folk art." He sat forward, keeping himself more alert. He couldn't dwell on his dilemma with Libby the whole blasted night, not if he expected to stay sane. "Historically, it's an old tradition brought to the States by African slaves. They believed that the bottles could capture roving or evil spirits. It's a common practice in the South now, especially in the Appalachians. That's where my Cherokee ancestors were from, so I adopted the tradition, too."

"It certainly makes this trail more scenic." Soft and pale, her hair blew around her face and shoulders. "Do you believe they can capture roving spirits?"

"I don't know." He'd never had any experience in that realm. "But a lot of people in the Appalachians still do. In hoodoo folklore, blue creates a crossroads between heaven and earth, with the elements of water and sky being blue."

"So that's why most of the bottles out here are blue?"

Matt nodded. "Blue feels right to me, too, because I'm from the Blue Clan. There are seven clans in Cherokee society."

"Are the other clans named after colors, too?"

"No. Some are animals and other things. There's a Wolf Clan. It's the largest one, but my family isn't in it. Clanship comes from one's mother. If you don't have a Cherokee mother, then you don't have a clan. But no one keeps formal or written records of clanships. You just have the knowledge of what you've been told."

"Kirby has a song called 'Cherokee Tears.' As I'm sure you know, it was written before he met your mother. So it wasn't inspired by her. But he told me that it's her favorite song of his."

Matt blew out his breath. There was no escaping Kirby, not where Libby was concerned. With that damned book of hers, she mentioned him every day.

"What do you think of 'Cherokee Tears'?" she asked.

He wanted to say that he hated it, but when he was a kid, it had been one of his favorites, too. "It's a powerful song, with it being about the Trail of Tears." How could Matt dislike a song that paid tribute to the Cherokee who'd been forced to leave their homeland

and migrate to Indian Territory, dying from hunger, exposure and disease along the way?

"You just said something nice about your dad."

"No, I didn't." He shrugged it off. "I said something nice about one of his songs."

"His music is what makes him who he is."

"What? A prick?"

She almost laughed. He could see her holding back. "You have his sense of humor, you know. He's prone to saying things like that, too."

"Oh, lucky me. A chip off the old smart-ass block."

She reached for his hand and took it in hers. "Lie down with me, Matt. Let's look at the stars from here."

"I don't know much about the constellations." He sank onto the straw beside her, letting himself enjoy the feeling of being near her, of holding hands. "Do you?"

She lifted her chin to the sky. "Not enough to point them out or recognize them."

"Maybe we can make up our own." He pointed to a grouping of stars, using their joined hands. "That looks like an X." He made the symbol in the air. "And those look like an O."

"So we can call them tic-tac-toe?"

"Or hugs and kisses." He turned his face toward hers. "It would be so easy to kiss you again." He paused for an excruciating second. "So damned easy."

She made a breathy sound. "We can't do it, Matt. We shouldn't."

"I know." Because easy would turn to difficult, and

they would struggle with it later. He lowered their hands, and their interlocked fingers drifted apart.

Silent, she sat upright, no longer looking at the stars.

He sat up, too, and with the banned kiss still on his mind, he said, "For the sake of us imagining how it would be, I'd be really gentle this time."

"You'd make me want more than a kiss." Her voice hitched on her words. "So much more."

His pulse jumped. "In the wagon? Like this?"

"It's a romantic setting."

"Not if we got caught. It wouldn't take much for our driver to notice the boss making out with one of the guests on the way to the marshmallow roast."

"I probably already look like we've been messing around. I've got straw in my hair." She blew a piece of it away from her face.

"Everyone has it all over them by the time these things are over." He threw a handful of it at her, showing her how it was done.

"Ooh, you." She grabbed a bunch and tossed it at him.

They laughed like a couple of kids having a pillow fight. Or what he assumed that would be like. He'd never actually been involved in a pillow fight before.

When they settled down, she asked, "What prompted you to build a recreational ranch?"

"I thought it would be a good investment, owning this much land and doing something with it. Of course, no one knows the truth about where I originally got the money. I told everyone that it came from my grandparents' life insurance policy and that my mother had put it in trust for me. I had to explain it somehow. Otherwise people would've wondered how I afforded all of this."

"So it was strictly an investment for you?"

"No. I liked the idea of creating a place for families to come, to have fun together. In the beginning, it gave me a sense of family, too."

"But it doesn't anymore?"

"Sometimes it does. But I've had the ranch for almost ten years now, so mostly it just makes me aware that I don't have a family of my own, other than when I was a stepfather to Sandy's kids."

"You miss them, don't you?"

"The kids? Yes, I do." Even if he hadn't been their dad for very long. "They're identical twins named Cassie and Kelly. They were seven when I married their mom."

She drew her knees up to her chest. The wagon was still rolling along. "Were you able to tell them apart?"

"Yes, but there were times they would try to trick me and insist that I was calling them by the wrong name. They thought it was funny to pretend they were the other sister." He smiled from the happy memory. "They already had that twin thing going on, with their own language and all of that."

She smiled, too. "Oh, that's cute. My maternal grandmother is a twin. She and her sister are fraternal, not identical, though."

"I always wished that I had a brother or sister. Kirby's

other sons didn't count." He clarified the difference. "I wanted a sibling who belonged to my mom, who lived with us, who was the same as me. Not some faraway strangers who belonged to my dad."

"Just remember that they're interested in you now."

"So you keep saying." But he wasn't going to subject himself to meeting them. He couldn't handle being around anyone who was close to his dad. Except for Libby, and that wasn't going in his favor, either. Not with how much he wanted her. "Was it tough for you being an only child?"

She nodded. "It was lonely sometimes."

He knew the isolated feeling. "Does Chance get lonely?" He was curious about her son.

"He has cousins on his dad's side who are around his age, so he has plenty of companionship. Mostly he gets lonely about not having a father."

Matt glanced out the wagon. They were nearing the spot where they would be having the marshmallow roast. "Maybe you'll get remarried someday."

"It's tough to think about that right now, especially when I haven't even dated anyone." She pressed a finger to her lips. "And the only man I've kissed so far is you."

"At least it's a start. At least you know what it's like to be attracted to someone again." He studied her in the moonlight. It was especially bright, and the stars they'd pointed out made it even brighter. "I haven't dated or been with anyone since my divorce. You probably already figured that out with the way I've been behaving around you. But you asked about it before and I never gave you a straight answer, so I'm telling you now."

"Thank you for opening up to me."

"I've been doing that a lot since I met you."

She put her hand on his knee, quickly, lightly, before she removed it. "We're becoming friends, Matt. Real friends."

"I think so, too. But that doesn't really help with the other stuff." The unfulfilled need, he thought, the fantasies, the desperation of wanting each other.

"I have to keep pretending when we're around other people that I don't have a crush on you. I'm going to have to do that when my mom gets here, too."

"Does your mom know that I'm Kirby's son? Have you told her?"

"Yes, she knows. My dad does, too. This was too big of a project for me to leave my parents out of it. I didn't want to have to lie about why I was spending time at a recreational ranch in Texas. I wanted the comfort of having my son here, too, along with my mom. I assured Kirby that my parents could be trusted to keep the information private. They would never leak anything to the press or try to sabotage the book."

"So how do they feel about all of this? Do they think Kirby is doing the right thing? Are they siding with him?"

"They aren't siding with anyone. It isn't their place to do that."

"Have they met Kirby?"

"No. But when I leave here and go to Kirby's place,

my mom and Chance are going with me, so Mom will get to meet him then. And so will Chance, of course. Chance knows he was named after one of Kirby's songs."

"Has he heard the song?"

"Oh, yes. He loves it. He listens to it all the time. But it will be great when he meets Kirby, because Kirby promised that he would serenade Chance with it."

Matt couldn't stand the thought of Libby returning to his dad's house. And now it bugged him that her mother and son would be going there, too, with Kirby playing the gracious host. But he wasn't going to let it ruin his night.

He was enjoying Libby's company far too much.

The marshmallow roast was warm and cozy with guests gathered around multiple fire pits. Everyone was making s'mores, squishing their toasted marshmallows between layers of chocolate and graham crackers. And there were campfire songs, particularly for the kids.

Libby sat next to Matt with a group of other people, all devouring their treats. One of the moms kept wiping her son's face and hands every few seconds. Libby wasn't that type of parent. She would simply let her son enjoy the goo.

She leaned over and said to Matt, "I wish Chance was here."

He replied, "Don't worry. We have these every week. You can do this again with him."

"Will you join us?" She wanted Matt to be there.

"Sure. I can do that."

"Thanks." She was eager for Chance and Matt to meet. As close as she was getting to Matt, she couldn't help feeling that way. Of course, it only heightened the complexity of her attraction to him, adding a gentler layer to it. But out here by the fire with other people around, they had to refrain from saying sensual things.

She noticed that Matt was on his second s'more, licking the messiness off his fingers. She smiled at him, doing her best to keep her thoughts clean. "You're enjoying that."

"Yes, ma'am, I am."

Libby managed another smile. He sounded like a full-blown Texan. He looked like one, too, his Western attire still covered with scattered blades of straw from the wagon. He hadn't bothered to dust himself off. The environment suited him, and so did the firelight, casting a glow on his already bronzed skin.

"Have you ever celebrated National S'mores Day?" he asked.

"I didn't even know there was such a thing."

"It's observed every August tenth. We have a big bash that day, with all sorts of fun and games. We even serve s'mores spaghetti."

She made a face. "Sorry, but that sounds awful."

"It's chocolate spaghetti, not real pasta."

She softened her expression, laughed a little. "You had me worried there for a second."

"Yeah, I'll bet." He laughed, too. "In the evening we have a cocktail party of sorts, with s'mores martinis for the adults and s'mores milkshakes for the kids."

"Oh, wow." Now he was talking her language. "I'd love to try one of those martinis. I like experimenting with different drinks."

"I can make you one sometime. I have the recipe down pat." He finished his treat. "Or maybe you can stay a bit longer and join in on the S'mores Day celebration."

"I can't do that. Not with my work schedule. I have to be in Nashville by then."

"Can't you at least try? I'm sure Chance would enjoy the celebration."

"Yes, I'm sure he would." But was there more to Matt's suggestion? Was he trying to keep her and Chance away from Kirby? She looked into his eyes. They were a deeper shade of amber, enhanced by the flames. He returned her gaze, and her pulse fluttered at her neck.

By now, one of the ranch attendants was leading everyone in another song, a silly tune that her son was sure to like. But Chance wasn't here right now, and Libby wasn't in the mood to sing. Not while she was looking at Matt.

She asked him, "Will you go for a walk with me?" She needed to talk to him in private.

He got to his feet and accompanied her.

Once they were a safe distance from the activity,

she unloaded the question that was on her mind. "Do you want me to stay because you're trying to keep me away from Kirby for as long as you can?"

"That's part of it. But I like having you around, even as difficult as it can be."

She fanned her face, feeling a heat that had nothing to do with the fire they'd walked away from. If anything, she should be cold, being so far away from it. "I like being around you, too. But I can't stay longer." She couldn't prolong her trip, even if she wanted to.

Matt blew out a breath. "Then I guess we'll just keep seeing each other and hanging out as friends while you're here."

"And suffer through the rest of it?"

"We don't have much of a choice in that regard, do we?"

"No, we don't." Just talking about it was bad enough. "I think we should invite some of the other guests to ride in our wagon on the way back."

"For appearance's sake? Or because you can't cope with being alone with me for the duration of the evening?"

"Both." If she climbed back into that straw-filled wagon with him, it would spark more of the feelings she was trying to avoid. And Libby was doing everything in her power to control her urges for Matt, and help him control his, too.

Nearly a week later, Libby sat alone on her porch, resting her weary bones. While hiking earlier, she'd taken a tumble and skinned her knee. It was a superficial injury, but it still hurt like the dickens.

Or maybe she was just missing Matt. He was out of town at a horse auction. He'd been gone since yesterday. She wasn't sure when he was coming back—tonight or maybe tomorrow. It depended on how his trip went.

Although their friendship was growing by leaps and bounds, forbidden urges continued to plague them. Since neither of them expected that to improve, they had learned to deal with it. Another thing that hadn't changed was Matt's unwillingness to participate in the book. He was still as reluctant as ever.

Eager to clear her mind, Libby adjusted the wooden chaise to a reclining position. Maybe she should take a nap and forget everything that was in her head.

She often dozed off at the beach, sinking into the sand on a towel. So why not sleep here on this late afternoon, surrounded by the Texas landscape? Besides, the chaise was padded with a nice, thick cushion.

Getting comfortable, she removed her lace-up boots and tucked her socks inside.

She closed her eyes, snuggled up and let herself drift.

The next thing she knew she was awakening from a floaty-feeling dream, with a make-believe Matt stroking her cheek. She murmured his name while he whispered hers.

"Libby. Are you okay?"

Suddenly he seemed too real to be coming from her

subconscious, his hand much too solid against her skin. In her haze, she forced her eyes open and squinted at the shadow in front of her, wondering if Matt was truly there.

"Is that you?" she asked.

"Yes, it's me," he answered. "What are you doing out here in the dark?"

"I was taking a nap." She sat up and blinked, trying to gauge how long she'd been out. She looked past him and noticed that the sky was riddled with stars. "What time is it?"

"It's just after nine."

She'd slept for hours. "I was really tired. I had an eventful afternoon. I scraped my knee when I was on a hike today."

"Were you with a group?"

"I was alone, but it was only a short hike." She knew better than to go deep into the hills by herself. She didn't know the area well enough.

"Come on." He sounded concerned. "I'll take you inside."

He lifted her up, cradling her in his arms before she could stop him. Not that she wanted to, but still...

"I can walk, Matt."

"Too late. I've already got you." He opened the front door of her cabin and flipped on the wall switch with his elbow, illuminating the living room.

As the light shone on his face, she noticed how tired he was. But he'd been on a road trip, a long drive from the ranch.

"You have beard stubble," she said. She'd only seen him clean-shaven. "It makes you look even more like a cowboy."

"I forgot my razor. But I don't like stubble. It itches."

She thought it was sexy, but she didn't say so. "You can put me down now."

He glanced at the sofa, but he bypassed it and headed for her room. Good heavens, she thought. He was taking her to bed. Not in a romantic sense, but it still made her feel that way.

He was good at maneuvering her in his arms. Too good, she decided. Her heart thumped, being this close to him.

He plopped her down on the unmade bed. She'd left a few clothes strewn about, too. She hadn't tidied up this morning. She'd also left her bedroom light on.

"Let me take a look at your knee." Instead of covering her with a blanket, he sat on the edge of the bed, leaving her exposed to his view.

"It's just a scrape." She was wearing shorts, the same pair she'd worn on the hike. "See? No big deal."

"You should have bandaged it."

"It's not that bad." She wiggled her toes, even if her feet had nothing to do with her injury.

"Even small cuts can get infected. Did you use an antibacterial on it?"

"No, but I poured water over it when it first happened."

He shook his head. "Let me take care of it properly for you."

"That isn't necessary."

His handsome features hardened. "Yes, it is."

With how persistent he was being, she quit her meager protests and let him take over.

He went into the bathroom and returned with a first-aid kit the ranch provided. She'd seen it under the sink, but hadn't thought to use it.

"You need to be more careful," he scolded. "The least you could have done was brought medical supplies with you."

"I didn't expect to fall."

He dabbed a liquid antiseptic on her knee, cleaning it his way. "You're not going hiking again by yourself."

"Wow. Listen to you." She smiled, hoping to defuse the situation. "Being the boss of me."

"That's right, I am. Next time you want to go on a hike, I'll go with you." He finished with her knee, placing a bandage on it. "You're not riding alone, either. You'll be going out with me, like we've been doing."

They'd been riding nearly every day this week, packing picnic lunches and eating by the creek. "You're just trying to hoard my time."

"So what if I am?" He closed the first-aid kit, snapping down on the plastic hinges a bit too noisily, and placed it on the nightstand.

She looked into his eyes, and he smoothed her hair away from her forehead. But he took his hand back soon enough. He seemed cautious about touching her in a way that hadn't been part of his doctoring.

"My mom and Lester are home," he said. "They just got back today. She called me while I was on the road."

Libby assumed that Lester was his mother's husband. Matt hadn't mentioned him by name until now. "Did you tell her about me?"

"Yes, I did, and she's interested in meeting you and discussing the book."

Her excitement mounted. "When do you think I'll get to talk to her?"

"Soon, I suspect. She seemed eager to meet you. I gave her your number."

"That was nice of you."

He frowned and pulled up the blanket, tucking it around her. "She asked for your number. I didn't offer it."

"I'm sorry if me meeting your mom causes you distress. But it's part of my job."

"Just keep me out of it, okay? I don't want to know what she tells you about my dad. Not unless she admits that she secretly hates him. But I doubt that's the direction it's going to take."

She fingered the blanket, the barrier he'd put between them. "You're the only one who hates him."

"Maybe I'm the only one with an ounce of brains around here." He cupped her chin, his expression softening. "You're a pretty little thorn in my side. You know that?"

Yes, she knew how she affected him. She leaned forward, put her arms around his neck and whispered, "Thanks for taking care of my knee."

"You're welcome." He nuzzled her cheek, his beard stubble rough against her skin. "I have to go. It's been a long night and I need to get some sleep."

She breathed him in, all the way to her soul. "I'd invite you to sleep here, but we both know the trouble that would get us into."

"The kind we can't undo once it's done. I'm going home like I'm supposed to." He moved away from her. "Do you want me to turn out the light?"

"I'm not ready for bed. I still have to change." She wasn't going to sleep in her clothes any more than he was likely to sleep in his. "Good night, Matt."

"Night." Before he left her room, he paused in the doorway and glanced back at her. One last time.

And then he was gone.

Six

The following morning, Libby got a call from Julie Clark-Simpson, Matt's mother, asking if they could meet that day.

She accepted the invitation, of course. She didn't tell Matt because he'd already left for work; his truck was gone from his driveway. But he was expecting his mother to contact her, so it wouldn't have come as a surprise to him, anyway. She just wished that he was as interested in the book as his mom was. That would certainly make things easier.

She headed over to the lodge, where Julie and her husband had their own suite of rooms in a quiet section of the east wing. Her anxiety mounting, she knocked on their door. A moment later, a tall, lanky man with weathered skin and thinning gray hair answered it. When he smiled, the crow's feet around his pale blue eyes crinkled. He was probably around Kirby's age, maybe sixty or so. But other than that, they weren't anything alike. This old cowboy had an unassuming disposition, whereas Kirby took center stage, even when he was trying to be humble.

"I'm Lester," he said. "Come on in. Julie will be with you shortly."

"Thank you." Libby entered the main room and glanced around. Amid the woodsy decor were magazines spread out on tabletops and plaid pillows tossed on the beige-and-brown sofa. Family photos decorated the fireplace mantel. Unable to help herself, she wandered over to them. Some were of Matt when he was a kid. A handsome boy, she thought, with familiar eyes.

"I didn't know him back then," Lester said, joining her at the mantel.

"But you know him now."

"Yes, I do. He's a good man, strong and kind and generous. He gave me a job when I needed one, and now I'm married to his mama." He gestured to a picture of an older couple. "Those are his grandparents. Julie's folks."

They looked happy, smiling in front of a Christmas tree, with opened gifts strewn on the floor at their feet. "It's too bad Matt never got to meet them. He told me that they died before he was born."

"A month apart. Can you imagine? Julie still misses them. It's a shame that they aren't here."

"How did they pass, so soon apart?"

"He was sick with cancer, and she had heart failure."

Libby studied the photo. Then she glanced at one of Matt's childhood pictures, where he sat outside on a fence rail, his boots layered with dust. She guessed him to be about seven, eight at the most. He was wearing a cowboy hat that was far too big for him. She realized it was the same hat his grandfather was wearing in the Christmas picture. She quickly surmised that his mother had probably given it to him as a keepsake.

Lester interrupted the quiet. "Can I offer you a snack? I've got a pot of coffee ready to go, and Julie made some bean bread this morning. That's why she's running late. She was bustling around the kitchen after she called you. She wanted to have something special for you to nibble on. It's a modern recipe based on an old Cherokee dish."

"That sounds great." Libby hadn't eaten breakfast. She'd been in too much of a hurry to come here. "I appreciate her thinking of me."

He led her to the kitchen. "Have a seat, and I'll get it for you."

She scooted onto one of the dining chairs. The table was round, scratched up a bit, with sturdy legs and a traditional Western star inlay pattern in the center. A matching hutch stood nearby.

"How do you take your coffee?" Lester asked.

"Truthfully, with anything you've got. Milk, cream, sugar, the fake sweeteners. I mix it altogether."

He chuckled and loaded up the table with her request. "Julie likes those flavored creamers. Hazelnut is her favorite." He set that out, as well.

"Thanks." Libby added a dollop to her cup, along with everything else. "When I first started drinking coffee, I couldn't decide how I liked it best, so I just went for it all."

"You sound like an adventurous gal." He placed a hearty piece of the bread in front of her, along with a napkin and a fork. "This is mostly made from corn, but you can see some of the pinto beans in there. We slather ours with butter," he said, offering it to her. "Some folks put sugar or syrup on theirs. It can also be eaten with meat and gravy."

She spread the butter and took a bite. "It's wonderful." The bread was thick and filling, with a homemade flavor. "I could make a meal out of this."

"Glad you like it. Julie is all aflutter about making a good impression on you. The book you're writing has got her coming and going. She barely slept a wink last night, and this morning she was rushing around like a headless chicken. She really wants Matt and his daddy to reconcile."

"Me, too." Libby continued eating. "I keep hoping he'll come around to the idea. But he hasn't yet."

"I'll leave that up to you and his mama." He patted the back of her chair. "I need to head off to work. But first, I'll check on Julie and let her know you're enjoying her bread."

"Boy, am I ever." By now, her plate was down to crumbs.

"If you're hankering for more, just help yourself." He gestured to the pan on the stove. "Eat as much as you want."

"Thanks. I will."

After he left the room, she went ahead and took another piece, then resumed her seat and glanced out the window. She liked the ambience at Matt's mother's suite.

When Julie dashed into the kitchen, Libby snapped to attention. She was a striking woman with straight, shoulder-length black hair and elegant bone structure. She wore a red blouse tucked into a pair of boot-cut jeans. Her only jewelry was her wedding band. Her makeup was minimal, mostly just a splash of cherry lip gloss that accentuated her blouse. She was in her early fifties, but looked much younger.

"I'm so sorry I'm late," she said. "But Lester already told you how scattered I've been since I found out about Kirby's biography." She paused as if to compose herself. "It really is a pleasure to meet you."

"It's wonderful to meet you, too." Libby stood to shake her hand. "The bread you made for me is delicious. I'm on my second helping."

"It's one of Matt's favorites. I was hoping you would like it, too."

"I definitely do." Libby sat down again. "I've become friends with your son, even if he doesn't approve of the book."

"Matt is touchy when it comes to his father. But it's been a long, hard road for him, having Kirby as his dad." Julie gestured to her coffee. "Would you like a refill?"

"Thanks, but I'm good. Your husband is quite the host."

"Lester is a sweetheart." Julie poured herself a cup and joined Libby at the table. "I'm lucky to have him." She added the hazelnut creamer and stirred it. "Before we get started, I want to clarify that I'm not ready to be interviewed. This is just an informal talk."

"Don't worry. I'm not going to rush you into anything." Libby understood that Matt's mother probably needed time to work through the past and consider the things she was willing to share. "I already explained over the phone that you'll have to sign a release for our conversations to be official and for me to record you. So for now you can just say whatever you want, and we can start over on another day when you're ready to do a formal interview. I want this to be a comfortable experience for you."

"Maybe I should start at the beginning, with how Kirby and I met and why I allowed myself to become his mistress." She glanced up from her cup. "If I tell you all of this now, I think it will be easier for me to repeat it later for the book."

"I agree." Libby wanted to hear as much as Matt's mother was willing to tell her, on and off the record.

"Okay, let's get started then," Julie said, nervously

clasping her hands in her lap. "I met Kirby when I was twenty. It was a difficult time in my life. I'd already lost my parents and was feeling terribly alone. After they passed, I moved in with my best friend and her boyfriend, but we had a falling out because I didn't get along with her boyfriend. So they asked me to leave their apartment."

Julie blew out an audible breath, as if the memory still pained her. "At the time I was in Austin, working at a horse boarding facility. I was also taking animal husbandry classes at a community college. I checked the bulletin boards at school and found a new roommate. After I moved in, she invited me to attend Kirby's concert with her. She'd won two free tickets from a local radio station and didn't have anyone to go with. She was new to the area and hadn't really made any friends."

Libby curiously asked, "Were you a fan of Kirby's?"

"I didn't know anything about him as a person, but I loved his music. It was especially exciting because the tickets included backstage passes, and it was the first time either of us had ever been backstage at a show."

Intrigued, Libby imagined the scenario in her mind, picturing Julia as a younger woman, en route to a concert that would ultimately change her life.

"After the show, we went to this area where there was food and drinks with some folding tables and chairs set up for the guests. Our passes weren't the all-access kind, where we could go back to the dressing rooms or anything like that. We were disappointed at first. We envisioned something grander."

Libby understood. She knew how the levels of backstage access worked and that it wasn't nearly as glamorous as people thought. "Did Kirby come out to where you were?"

"It took a while, but he finally did. And then he kept looking over and smiling at us, flirting, if you will. But he didn't approach us, and we were too shy to go over to him. He was surrounded by other people."

"So how did you meet him?"

"After he went back to his dressing room, his manager came over to us and said that Kirby was having a party the following night at his hotel and that we were invited. But my roommate couldn't go. She was going out of town for a family wedding that weekend. I debated what to do, and if I was brave enough to attend Kirby's party by myself."

"I assume that you were."

Julie nodded. "It was the scariest thing I'd ever done. Kirby had a suite that overlooked the city, and I went traipsing up there, this little nobody, totally out of my element. I was too nervous to mingle. All I wanted was to get out of there. And just as I was planning on leaving, Kirby came up to me. He told me that he'd been looking for me and my friend, hoping that we came. But mostly it was me he wanted to see. I was the reason he invited us."

Here was where the plot thickened, Libby thought.

A range of emotions crossed Julie's face. She sat quietly for a moment before she said, "He was the most compelling man I'd ever met, so rough and wild and charming. He wasn't partial to groupies or women who threw themselves at him. He liked that I was a regular girl." A frown creased her brow. "He told me that he was married, but that he and his wife had an understanding. I should have walked away then. Being with a married man, under any circumstances, wasn't within my moral compass. But God forgive me, I got swept up in it."

"How often did you see him after that?"

"Just here and there. He would send me airline tickets so I could meet him on the road. I kept it from my roommate. I didn't want her to know I was sleeping with a married man. In fact, I lied and told her that I never went to the party. She had no idea that I'd even met Kirby. I pretended that I had out-of-town jobs on the weekends I was gone. After a while, it didn't matter because she went back to the little farm town in Iowa where she was from, and I moved into a big fancy apartment that Kirby paid for. He pretty much paid for everything, so I quit my job and went to school full-time. But I had to be available whenever he needed me. I kept telling myself that it didn't matter that he was married or that he had two small boys. According to my newfound rationale, I wasn't a home wrecker. He'd told me that his wife's only stipulation in their arrangement was that he didn't have any kids with anyone except her, so I wasn't breaking any of their rules." Julie sighed. "About a year later, I got pregnant."

Silent, Libby nodded.

Julie shifted in her seat. "I was on the Pill, and I was diligent about taking it. I never missed a dose. So the best I can figure is that I threw it up on one of the nights when I had too much wine with Kirby. I've never been much of a drinker, and I don't handle alcohol very well."

"How did Kirby react when you told him about the baby?" About Matt, Libby thought.

"He went nuts, freaking out about what to do. He didn't ask me to terminate the pregnancy because he knew that wasn't an option for me, not with my spiritual beliefs. Finally, he said that we would just have to keep it a secret so his wife never found out. And that's what we did, for many, many years." Tension edged Julie's voice. "I wasn't Kirby's only mistress. But eventually, I was the one who ended his marriage. Melinda divorced him when she discovered Matt's existence."

"I know, but she's friends with Kirby again. In fact, she wants to meet Matt. She's interested in knowing him. So are his brothers."

"Really? Oh, thank goodness." Julie relaxed a bit. "My guilt has been eating away at me all these years, with the way I hurt her and her children. I realize it was Kirby who kept the truth from them, but I was still part of the lie."

"Matt told me how faithful you were to Kirby. The

years you spent being loyal to him, staying up at night, waiting for him to visit."

"It sounds crazy when I look back on it. But he was the father of my child, and I loved him as much as a woman can love a man who's sharing himself with other women. I think he loved me, too, in his own needy way. But he was as guilty as I was, so our relationship never really made much sense. Plus there were his drug and alcohol problems. He had all sorts of demons."

"He's conquered most of them, except for the way he abandoned Matt. Aside from this book, Kirby doesn't know what else to do to get Matt's attention."

"Matt has other issues. Not only what he suffered from Kirby."

"I'm aware of his divorce and how it affected him." Libby knew he was more than just Kirby's secret son.

Julie seemed surprised, her cup coming to a halt midway to her mouth. "He told you about Sandy and her children?"

"Yes, and I've been telling him about my deceased husband and my son. I'm a widow, too."

"Oh, my." Julie was still holding her cup in the same position, without drinking, without moving. "I'm so sorry you lost someone you loved." Her gaze turned soft and searching. "I'm glad you're friends with my son. That you're confiding in each other."

"I'm glad, too." But there was more to Libby's feelings for Matt than she was letting on: the ever-raging battle of their attraction. She couldn't say that to his mother.

"I'm convinced that Matt reconciling with his father is the right thing to do. I think it'll help Matt move on with his life."

"I agree. But so far I haven't been able to bring him around to my way of thinking."

"You must be more influential than you're giving yourself credit for or Matt wouldn't have told you so many personal things about himself. He doesn't do that with just anyone."

"We've established a deep rapport." But a confusing one, too. Nothing in her research had prepared her for being as attached to Matt as she was. But again, she didn't reveal that to his mother. Libby was being cautious, keeping her romantic notions to herself.

At ten o'clock that night, Libby climbed out of a long, warm bath and put on a pair of blue silk pajamas. Her hair was pinned up, with damp tendrils curling around her face.

A knock sounded on her door, and she assumed it was Matt. She hadn't seen him all day. Besides, who else would show up at her cabin like this?

Sure enough, when she opened the door, there he was, standing under the porch light, his T-shirt stretched across his shoulders and his jeans fitting in all the right places.

He gazed at her pajamas. "Oh, I'm sorry. Were you on your way to bed?"

"Not yet. I just was going to make a cup of herb tea. But now that you're here, why don't you come and join me?" She couldn't very well send him away.

"Okay." He crossed the threshold. "I just got off work. I was swamped this evening, but I wanted to see how your knee was doing."

"It's fine. Hardly noticeable anymore." Unlike the pounding of her heart. Last night he'd carried her to bed to doctor her knee, and tonight he was here again, checking up on her.

He followed her into the kitchen, and she put the water on to boil. While they waited, he said, "Those match your eyes."

"What does?"

"Your pj's."

Her breath lodged in her throat. She wasn't wearing a bra, and now her nipples were getting hard—a reaction to being around him. She wished the water would hurry up and boil.

He shifted his stance. "That color looks pretty on you."

"Thank you." She reached up to remove the pins from her hair and let it fall. "I forgot to take my hair down after I got out of the bath." She pulled some long strands forward, trying to camouflage the outline of her nipples.

Her hair wasn't covering her all the way, but he

didn't appear to notice her dilemma. Or he was pretending not to. She could have kissed him for that. Well, maybe not kissed him, exactly. Not for real, anyway.

He said, "I don't drink tea very often."

She removed two plain white cups from the cabinet, glad that he'd said something mundane. She could handle normal, everyday conversation. "I prefer coffee, but herb tea is nice at night."

"I think the water is ready."

Libby glanced at the pot. It was just starting to bubble. "You're right." She put the tea bags in their cups and poured the water. "Do you want sugar or anything?"

"No, thanks. It'll be fine the way it is."

"For me, too."

"You don't put all sorts of junk in your tea?"

"I just do that to my coffee." She dunked her tea bag, making the liquid stronger and darker.

Matt did the same thing. Then they both removed the bags and set them in the sink.

He sipped his tea first. "This tastes pretty good. It smells good, too." In a quiet voice, he added, "So do you, Libby. Like flowers or something."

Heat rose in her cheeks, and it wasn't just from her teacup. Damn him for putting her in this predicament. He was back to saying things she wished he wouldn't say.

He continued, "On the first night we danced together, you smelled lemony. And on the day you came to my place dressed in that motorcycle-type gear, you smelled spicy."

"I like to change up my fragrances." Tonight she'd used rose-scented bath salts.

"It all works on you." He glanced toward the living room. "Should we sit a spell?"

She nodded. Standing in the kitchen talking about how good she smelled certainly wasn't helping the situation.

They went over to the sofa and sat down. Before he said something else that disturbed her, she asked, "Did your mother tell you that I met with her this morning?"

"No, she didn't." He put his cup on the end table next to him. "I haven't seen her today." Frowning, he asked, "How did it go?"

"It was an informal discussion. Not an interview."

"Is she going to let you interview her?"

"Yes. She just needs a bit of time to think about how much information she's willing to share."

"What did she share with you today?"

Libby cocked her head. "I thought you didn't want me to tell you."

"You're right, I don't. I just got curious for a second. But forget I asked." He waved away his interest. "I don't want to hear about my mom's relationship with Kirby. I lived through enough of it already. It'll just bug me all over again."

Libby agreed that this wasn't the time to discuss

it. But since neither of them could think of anything else to say, they slipped into a bout of painfully awkward silence.

He looked into her eyes, capturing her gaze with his, and that was all it took for the sexual awareness to come back.

Her pulse ticked like a time bomb. His was probably doing the same. Now what were they supposed to do? Stare at each other half the night, with heat zigzagging between them?

She'd never been so frazzled in all her life.

Seven

When Libby finally summoned the strength to break eye contact, the only thing she managed to do was glance down at Matt's jeans. She noticed how the denim was worn and faded at the seams, with tiny gold threads coming loose. It seemed symbolic, somehow. She was unraveling, too.

He breathed roughly, heavily. "I should probably go home."

He definitely should. But she didn't want him to leave. As overwhelming as it was, she longed to keep him as close as she could, for as long as she could. Clearly, she was losing her mind, going time-bomb crazy. Her pulse was still ticking away.

She forced herself to say, "You can stay awhile. We'll get through it."

"Will we really?" he asked.

She lifted her gaze to his face, to his black hair. He was as dark and thrilling as a man could be. If she inhaled deeply enough she could even smell the ranch, the hay and horses, on his skin. She imagined it mingling with the rose-soft scent of her bath salts.

He cleared his throat. Or tried to. "If I stay, I'm just going to sit here and fantasize about putting my hands all over you."

She fidgeted with her top, where her nipples were still pressing against the fabric. "That's what I do, especially when I'm in bed. I think about you touching me."

He scooted closer to her, his leg nearly bumping hers. "You're tempting me to make our fantasies come true, but I know I'm not supposed to."

She should end this now and tell him to go home. Tell him that he was right about leaving. But it wouldn't change anything. She would just wake up tomorrow feeling the same way.

"Maybe we should stop fighting it," she said. Maybe it was insane to think they could keep drowning in desire and not do anything about it. "Maybe you should just stay the night."

There. She'd made the decision.

He seemed ready to pounce, his reflexes on carnal alert. But he hesitated and asked, "Are you sure?"

"I'm positive." Or as positive as she could be with the desire that was spiraling through her veins and clouding her judgment. "Except that we need to use protection, and I certainly don't have any."

"I have some. But they're—"

"You don't have to explain." She didn't need to know why he was carrying condoms around, if they were tucked away in his wallet from when he was married or placed there after the divorce. His celibacy was about to be broken, either way.

She reached for him, and he reacted quickly. He pushed her down on the couch, climbed on top of her and kissed her.

Hotly. Roughly. Passionately.

He undid her top, opening the first three buttons and slipping his hands inside the material to cup her breasts. He thumbed her nipples, and she lifted her hips and rubbed against his fly, wanting to feel the hardness beneath his zipper.

He kissed his way to her neck and scraped her with his teeth. He went lower, nibbling at her collarbone.

When he undid the rest of her buttons and opened her top all the way, she caught her breath. He took one of her nipples straight into his mouth.

Libby thrust her hands into his hair, tugging on the short, choppy strands. He lowered a roving hand into her pajama bottoms, pushed past her panties and touched her in the most intimate of places. He used his fingers, toying with her senses.

She blinked through the haze and focused on the beamed ceiling dappled in light. Was she actually sprawled out on the sofa, with Matt doing wicked things to her? "If you keep doing that, I'm going to come."

"That's the idea." He moved his mouth to her other nipple, his hand still wedged in her panties.

She wanted to feel him up, too, but she couldn't. She was pinned beneath him, his weight holding her in place. Was this how women felt in bondage situations? Was this why they enjoyed it, giving themselves over to the men who dominated them?

Libby was giving herself over to Matt. He could do whatever he wanted, and she would let him. Every pull of his mouth, every slick rub of his hand, every hot, erotic sensation made her wonderfully weak. Or maybe they were making her sinfully strong.

Whatever it was, he commanded her to his will. He tugged her pajama bottoms past her hips, along with her panties, removing them and leaving her bare to his touch. In the next wild-hearted instant, he went down on her, burying his face between her legs.

She gazed up at the ceiling again, afraid the roof was going to crash and tumble down on her. It was like being in the middle of an earthquake. Or maybe it was more like a tornado, with the way she was twisting and turning and rocking against Matt. Had she ever been this wet, this warm or this eager to be pleasured? She couldn't have stopped him if she tried. His tongue was on her trigger.

Libby convulsed when she came, every nerve ending in her body fusing in fire. She curled her toes into the couch; she dragged oxygen into her lungs; she did whatever she could to survive it.

After the climax ended, she lay there, dazed from the feeling. She meant to smile at Matt, but then he sat up and said, "Now I really do have to go home."

"You're leaving?" After what he'd just done to her? She reached for her panties and put them back on, trapped in a sudden wave of self-consciousness. "Why?"

"To get the protection. It's at my cabin." He shook his head, as if he was confused. "And why are you covering yourself up?"

She let out the breath she'd been holding. "I felt weird sitting here with no underwear on."

"But why?"

"I didn't understand why you were going home. I assumed you had the protection on you." A mistake, obviously, since she hadn't let him explain earlier.

A muscle twitched in his jaw. "Did you think I was going home for good?"

"I wasn't sure."

"I would never leave in the middle of us being together. I want to make love with you so damned bad."

Excited by his admission, she squeezed her thighs together. "Then hurry back and take me to bed."

"I will. But are you sure you're going to be okay with this?"

"I'm going to be fine, Matt."

"Okay, but you seem sort of vulnerable, even now."

"That's because of us getting our wires crossed." She leaned forward, kissing him, showing him that she wasn't a damsel in distress. She wasn't sure how convincing she was, because he was very gentle as he returned her affection.

She refused to swoon, to get all girlie and such. Instead, she pushed him away and said, "Go. Before I start biting you."

"Oh, yeah?" He grabbed her and set her on her feet. "Just wait here for me, exactly as you are."

"Hot and ready for you?" She would wait the entire night if she had to. "That's not a problem." Not as much as she wanted him.

Matt dashed over to his cabin, went into his bedroom, grabbed a handful of condoms and stuffed them in his pocket.

Was he doing the right thing? Was Libby really going to be okay? She insisted that having sex with him wasn't going to mess with her emotions, and he hoped that was true. He knew how quickly a woman could cry. Or curl into a ball. Or stare into space, wishing her husband was still alive, the way Sandy had.

He went outside and stood on his porch, breathing in the night air. If only Libby didn't have the pain of being a widow. But he couldn't change who she was, any more than he could change who he was.

He returned to her cabin and opened her door. She stood in the same spot, waiting for him, just as he'd asked her to.

"I'm ready," he said.

"Then let's do this." She went over to him, took his

hand and led him to her bedroom, where a night-light was already burning, soft and low.

He wondered what her bedroom was like at her house in California. But he knew he was never going to find out. His affair with Libby would be limited to Texas, to the remaining time she was here.

He removed the condoms from his pocket and tossed them onto the nightstand. The packets glittered as they scattered on the wood surface. "I figured it wouldn't hurt to have extras."

"It won't hurt at all." She gazed at him from beneath her lashes. "Is your heart beating as fast as mine?"

"It depends on how fast yours is going." His was thumping like a monster rattling its cage. He removed his boots then peeled off his T-shirt, pulling it over his head and tossing it aside. He undid the top button on his jeans, too, relieving the pressure. He was getting hard just standing here, thinking about being with her.

She moved closer, running her hand down his stomach, then past his navel, heading farther and farther south. A sound of pleasure erupted from his throat and escaped his lips. He loved being steeped in her foreplay.

She unzipped his jeans, reached into his pants and stroked him. He could have come on the spot. But he didn't, of course. He wasn't a kid and this wasn't his first rodeo. He was a grown man with plenty of control.

"I could get on my knees for you," she said.

Holy hell. He jerked forward. "Let's save that for

another time." Control aside, he wanted this to last as long as it possibly could.

"But you already did it to me."

"That's different."

"It's a double standard, that's what it is."

He kissed her, just to shut her up. Or maybe he did it because he was desperate to put his tongue in her mouth.

Yeah, he thought. It was as primal and basic as that.

In a sensual blur, they got into bed, tousling the covers and kissing some more. Somehow, he managed to shed the rest of his clothes. She got rid of what was left of hers, too.

Finally, they were naked together, with lust curling low in his belly. She was wet and ready and grinding against him.

Matt took a condom off the nightstand and tore into the package. She watched as he put on the protection.

Then all at once, he pushed himself inside her, air hissing between his teeth. She wrapped her legs around him, and he began to thrust with a strong rocking motion.

He didn't stay on top for long. He shifted to another position, rolling her over so she was straddling him.

"Now you can show me what kind of cowgirl you are," he said, poking fun at all of the times he'd treated her like a city girl.

She tossed her head and smiled. "I'll just go for a nice, long, hard ride."

"Damn right, you will." Encouraging her to do just that, he circled his hands around her waist.

She impaled herself, taking him deep. Matt's eyes nearly rolled to the back of his head. She moved up and down, her skin glowing in the light.

She was the most provocative cowgirl he'd ever seen, and for now she was his. He liked being in possession of her. It almost made him feel married again.

Almost, he told himself. There was more to marriage than hot-blooded, hip-thrusting sex. If it had been that easy, he would still have a wife.

"Kiss me," he said, giving her a passionate order.

She leaned forward and bit him, making good on her threat from earlier. He growled and nipped her right back. But they kissed, too, as roughly as they could.

He tightened his grip on her. A few bewitching minutes later, he shifted their positions again. He wanted to finish while he was on top.

He practically pounded her into the bed, moving fast and hard. It was dangerously wild. He twined her hair around his fingers, tugging on the wavy blond strands.

Her big blue eyes bored into his. She looked beautifully, savagely ravished, her skin flushed with animalistic fever. Her appetite was as feral as his.

"I'll hold you when it's over," he said.

She dug her nails into his shoulders, leaving half-moon marks on his skin. "I'm not concerned about that."

"I am." He wanted the afterglow to mean something, not be mired in regret. But for now he just needed to come. And make her come, too. Matt was determined for it all to happen at the same time.

And it did. So help him, it did.

He used his fingers to guide her to her climax. He didn't need any more coaxing. He closed his eyes and let himself explode into a thousand jagged pieces.

With Libby shattering beneath him.

Libby sank into the bed, her limbs wobbly, her body spent.

Matt got up to discard the condom, and when he returned, he took her in his arms. Holding her, as he'd told her he would.

"You don't have to baby me," she said.

"I'm not babying you. I'm treating you like I'm supposed to."

"I'm not going to break." She didn't need as much attention as he was giving her. She'd already told him, countless times, that she wasn't going to get emotional over sleeping with him. So why did he have to keep pushing the issue? "I'm not the type you have to fuss over."

"So Becker never held you after sex?"

"Of course he did." And now the memory was jabbing her straight in the heart. But so was Matt's concern for her. She couldn't bear the cautious way he was looking at her. "But not every time. Sometimes we just rolled over and went to sleep."

He frowned. "So that's what you want me to do? To roll over and let you sleep?"

She sighed, realizing that she didn't actually know what she wanted. This was strangely new to her. As amazing as it was, there was no familiarity in being with Matt. He wasn't her boyfriend or her husband or the father of her child. There was no commitment between them.

"You can hold me," she said, doing her darnedest to figure it out, to let it flow, to make it as natural as it could be. "But not because I'm going to fall apart or because you think it's your obligation. Just do it because it feels nice."

"It does feel nice." He tucked her in the crook of his arm. "Everything with you does."

Libby snuggled closer to him, and suddenly this mattered far more than she could say. The warmth and kindness he was offering, the romantic way in which he wrapped her in his embrace. She put her head against his chest and listened to the beat of his heart. Being naked with him, warm and toasty in her bed, was heaven on earth.

But was that a good thing? she asked herself. Or would it only serve to make her more attached to him than she should be?

"I'm going to take the day off tomorrow," he said.

Fascinated with his body, with how big and strong it was against hers, she skimmed her fingers along his abs. "To hang out with me?"

"Absolutely. I won't be able to work with you on my mind. It'll drive me batty."

She stopped just shy of moving her hand lower, of making him hard, of arousing him again, even though she wanted to. "How long are we going to do this?"

"Do what? Have sex?" He nuzzled her cheek. "For as long as you're at the ranch." He nipped her earlobe, his voice sending chills up her spine. "I'm game if you are."

She shivered from his touch, his playfulness, his sexiness. "My mother and Chance will be here soon. It'll be difficult for us to be together then."

"We'll just do the best we can." He covered her hand with his and nudged it between his legs, encouraging her to stroke him, just the way she wanted to.

She rubbed her thumb over the tip, memorizing the shape of him, creating familiarity. "Are we making up for lost time already?"

"Yes, ma'am." He shifted onto his side. "I'm going to be ready to go again."

"I can tell." His erection was growing, popping up and pressing between them. "And just so you know, I like it when you call me ma'am. It's so country boy of you."

"That's what I am. A guy who owns a ranch."

He was also the abandoned son of a celebrity and the former husband of a lost and lonely widow. Those were major facets of Matt's personality. But Libby didn't say that out loud. They both already knew the effect Kirby's betrayal and Sandy's grief had on him.

"What are you thinking about?" he asked, watching her through curious eyes.

"Nothing," she lied. "I just want you inside me again."

"I'm here for whatever you want." He kissed her, long and sweet and slow.

Libby sighed. Maybe it wasn't so bad being with a man who understood the emotional needs of a woman, who cared so deeply about giving his partner comfort. Even if Libby wasn't broken inside, she still had moments of feeling lost and lonely, too. If she didn't, she wouldn't be human.

"You're going to have to hold me again afterward," she said. "I want to sleep in your arms."

"I can make that happen." He climbed on top of her, and they kissed some more.

His lips were utterly delicious. She couldn't get enough of him. He removed a condom from the nightstand. But she took it from him and opened the packet, fitting him with the protection. She wanted any and every excuse to touch him.

This time when they made love, it was soft and dreamy. He caressed her, and she smiled at him. They whispered words of encouragement, of tenderness, of togetherness.

It wasn't going to last forever. But for now, it was what Libby needed.

Matt had been awake for hours, watching Libby sleep.

Her face, her features fascinated him. She could

look innocent or sultry, depending on how she presented herself. At the moment, she struck him as both. A naughty angel, he thought, with her night-tousled hair strewn across a pillow and the covers bunched around her naked body.

He opened the blinds a crack, letting in more light and giving him a sunnier view of her.

Itching to touch her, he leaned over and skimmed his knuckles, ever so softly, along her jaw.

A second later, he took his hand away and glanced at the clock. It was early, but he was accustomed to ranch hours.

Eventually, Matt got out of bed. He grabbed his jeans off the floor and put them on. Libby's pajama top and panties were on the floor, too.

He went into the bathroom, put some toothpaste on his finger and rubbed it over his teeth. He rinsed and spit. It was the best he could do under the circumstances.

He also needed a shower, but he would rather take one with Libby, so he decided to wait until she was up. He intended to make the most of the time they had left, starting with today.

Matt headed for the kitchen to make a pot of coffee. He brewed it strong and dark and poured himself a cup.

Curious about Libby's domestic habits, he opened the fridge, taking inventory of its contents. Although the ranch offered meals at the lodge, guests could order groceries from the local market and have them delivered. Of course, they could go into town for their own supplies, too. But Libby didn't do that. The only time she'd been to town, as far as he knew, was when he'd taken her there.

Did she like to cook? he wondered. For now, she had mostly fruits, salad stuff and sandwich fixings on hand. But she was by herself. It might be different once her mother and son arrived.

"Good morning," Libby said from behind him.

He closed the fridge. Apparently she was up and about now. He turned around. She was delightfully disheveled, wrapped in a terry-cloth robe embroidered with the Flying Creek Ranch logo.

"Are you hungry?" she asked.

"I wasn't looking for anything to eat."

"Then what were you doing?"

"Truthfully, I was just snooping around."

She cocked her head. "To see what my food preferences are? That's not very exciting."

To him, it was. He figured it was the closest he was going to get to seeing how she lived, short of going to California.

He gestured to her robe. "What have you got on under that thing?"

Her lips curved into a siren's smile. "Nothing."

"Oh, yeah. Would you care to show me?"

"I could, I suppose."

With a flirty air, she flashed him, opening and closing the robe too damned quickly. He barely got to see a smidgen of skin.

He reached for his coffee. "That's not fair."

"It's what you get, cowboy, at this time of the morning." She came closer and peered into his cup. "That looks like motor oil."

"Want to be daring and try it?" He held it under her nose. "Without any of the sweet and creamy junk you put in yours?"

"I'll pass." She glanced down, past his cup. "You forgot to button your jeans."

He glanced down, too. "At least I zipped them. Do you want to go to my house?"

"To your cabin?"

"To the house I built." He wanted Libby to see it for what it was—the big, sprawling place that used to be his home. As close as they'd become, it seemed like the thing to do.

Her eyes turned bright. "I'd love to go there with you. Should we go now? I can hurry and get dressed."

He figured she would jump at the chance. She was always eager to learn more about him. She'd come to the ranch to meet him, after all, and try to interview him for Kirby's biography.

He put his coffee on the counter. Taking her to his house had nothing to do with the book. Nothing about them becoming lovers did.

"Here's the deal," he said. "We're not getting dressed or going anywhere. Not until we get naked again."

She pulled a cute face. "Is that so?"

"Yes, *ma'am*." He put a sexy emphasis on the last part because she'd told him that she liked him calling her that, and he wanted to please her and tease her and make her smile. "You and I are going to get squeaky clean together."

She laughed. "Is that an invitation to shower with you?"

"You bet it is." He kissed her, tasting a fresh burst of mint on her lips. Apparently she'd brushed her teeth before she came stumbling in here. She might have combed her hair, too. With that long, tumbling mane of hers, it was hard to tell.

Either way, he could have kissed her to the sun and back. Or to the moon. Or the stars. Wherever it took him.

After they separated, she said, "You'll have to use the soap the ranch gives its guests. If you use mine, you'll smell like a girl."

"Yeah, you and all those fancy scents of yours. Come on." He tugged on the belt of her robe, using it as leverage before he hauled her off to the shower.

And stripped her bare.

Eight

Libby and Matt took turns beneath the spray of water. She went first, using the citrus body wash and shampoo she'd brought from home. By the time she was done, she would probably smell like lemon meringue pie. Somehow she doubted that Matt would mind. He enjoyed her fragrances.

He stood back and watched. In the oversize bathtub doubling as a shower stall, he had plenty of room to observe, to be a tall, dark, silent voyeur. He had a condom handy, but for now they didn't need it. That would come later, Libby thought.

She felt downright scandalous, running her hands over her own body while Matt pierced her with his gaze. Clearly, he was gaining gratification from watching her. He was already half aroused, his erection jutting against his stomach. Every so often, he took a deep and ragged breath, inhaling the scented steam that rose in the air.

Libby took special care washing her breasts, over and around her nipples. Matt kept watching. With deliberate slowness, she moved lower, using the liquid soap between her thighs.

"Tease," he said.

"My, my." She checked out his muscle-roped body. He was nearly fully aroused now. "Look at the state you're in."

"Yeah, and who made me this way?"

She fluttered her lashes. "Was it little ole me?" She stepped out from under the showerhead, making room for him. "I'm done. You can take your turn now."

He switched places with her. But he didn't put on a show the way she did. He moved at a quick and efficient pace, lathering with the plain white bar of soap that was compliments of his ranch. Just as she'd suggested.

"I think you need to slow down a bit." She took the soap from him. "Why don't you let me help?" She focused mostly on his erection, using her hands, making him bigger and harder.

"Is that the only part of me you're going to touch?" he asked in a gruff voice.

"It is for now." She dropped to her knees. Heart skipping a beat, she looked up at him, waiting to see how he would react.

"Libby." His voice turned even huskier. "What am I going to do with you?"

"You're going to enjoy having me around."

His fingertips skimmed her cheek. "I should stop you."

"You already stopped me last night. You have to be good today."

"I think it's more like being bad."

Good. Bad. It was all the same to her. She took him in her mouth, causing his entire body to shiver. He latched onto her wet hair, twining it around his fingers.

When he rocked his hips, he created a motion that drove her forward, inspiring her to take him deeper.

All the way to the back of her throat.

He gripped her scalp, his hands tight upon her head. He was definitely being good. Or bad. Or whatever either of them chose to call it. He'd fallen under the spell she'd hoped to cast.

Steam continued to rise. The water was still running, too. It splashed from the showerhead, bouncing off Libby's breasts, running down her stomach and pooling around her knees. She imagined how erotic she must look to Matt, doing what she was doing to him. Excitement mounted between them. Giving him pleasure was turning her on, too.

He moved in and out of her mouth, encouraging her to keep going, but when he reached a point where he could no longer endure it, he insisted that she stop. That he needed her. That he wanted her. That he couldn't wait.

Empowered by his urgency, Libby smiled and climbed to her feet. In a matter of seconds, he put on the protection and entered her so hard, she almost banged her head.

So much for being smug.

She flung her arms around his neck, but they struggled to find their rhythm. He was too tall for her to meet his thrusts and for him to stay inside.

Finally, he turned her around and positioned her in front of him. She bent forward and put her palms flat against the wall, using it to brace herself. She also lifted one of her legs onto the side of the tub. It was just what they needed to get around their height difference.

He grabbed her hips and went to town. She moaned, and he growled in her ear. She loved the sounds he made during sex. She loved how he held her afterward, too—making her feel safe, as if nothing tragic would ever happen to her again.

She gulped a breath of steam. The tub was ridiculously foggy now. And so was her brain. Deep down, she knew that Matt didn't have the power to shelter her from the world. It just seemed as if he did.

This kind, beautiful man. This fantasy cowboy of hers.

He was pushing her toward an orgasm. Already he knew what to do to make her come, as their bodies slapped together with such heat that it made her head swim. She pitched forward, giving in to the passion.

After it was over, after he came, too, she turned

around and sagged against him, falling into his arms and letting him be her protector. Or at least the warm, sweet illusion of one.

After Matt and Libby got dressed and made instant oatmeal for breakfast, he took her to the house he'd built. But as soon as they arrived, he questioned his reasoning for bringing her here. This house wasn't just the place where he'd lived with Sandy and the twins. It held a frustrating connection to Kirby, too.

"The architecture is beautiful," Libby said as they exited his truck and stood in the yard.

"I wanted it to be rustic, but modern, too, to fit with the rest of the ranch." The grounds were elegantly landscaped, with acres of grass and towering trees.

"It looks like a country mansion."

He shrugged, making light of its size. "When I built it, I was planning on having a family someday." He unlocked the door, and they entered the living room. Everything was still fully furnished, exactly the same as when he'd lived here. "When I moved into the cabin where I am now, all I took were a few suitcases."

She glanced around. "You have impeccable taste."

"I didn't do this myself. I used a decorator, the same one who decorated the lodge and the cabins. But I wanted it to have a homey feeling, with the brick walls and limestone floors. Or my kind of homey, I guess. Even with how big it is."

They wandered into the kitchen, and she said, "It

would be fun to cook in here. You've got a wonderful setup."

"I've got a great patio out back for barbecuing, too." He leaned against the counter, giving her the full story. "I did have a family in mind when I built this place, but there was a part of me that was trying to compete with Kirby, too. I knew that he had a compound in Nashville, and I wanted to have something grand, too. I realize this is nowhere near what he has, but it made me feel better to spoil myself." He made a tight face. "And then later, it didn't matter. A house is just a house. It's people who make it a home."

"Some guys would have blown their trust fund on frivolous things. You built a recreational ranch, along with a home for yourself. There's nothing wrong with that."

"At first I wanted to throw the money back in Kirby's face. Or do something frivolous with it, as you said. But then I decided that after I got the ranch going, after it was a success, I would return the money to the trust. I wanted Kirby to know that I was making it on my own and I was never going to touch his money again." He paused and added, "I also wanted to work toward having a wife and kids someday. Needless to say, my divorce hit me hard. But I'm trying to get over it."

Libby stood near a window, where sunlight danced through the glass. "By having an affair with me?"

"It is a damn fine affair." He admired the way the sun highlighted the whiteness of her hair, giving her a snow-in-the-summer quality. "We should have given in sooner than we did."

"At least we're doing something about it now."

He thought about what she'd done to him in the shower. "I'll say." A second later, he got a brainstorm. "We should sleep here tonight."

She gaped at him. "Does that mean that you're moving back in? Making this your home again?"

"I don't know. Maybe." He didn't want to make a snap decision about that. "But for now, it's better than us bed-hopping between our cabins."

"It would definitely be more convenient."

"Then why don't you stay here for the duration of your trip? We can both move our stuff in today. Your mom and Chance can stay here, too. I've got plenty of room for all of you."

She gaped at him again. "I can't share a room with you while they're here."

"That wasn't what I was suggesting." He would never put her in that position. "You'd be sleeping in one of the guest rooms by then."

"I don't know if me staying here with my family is a good idea. It might be better for me to keep my cabin."

Frustrated by her reluctance, he scowled. "After you leave here, you're taking them with you to Kirby's. So why does he get to be their host, but you won't let me do it?"

"You're right. It isn't fair. But I still don't think it's a good idea."

"Come on, Libby. I want to get to know your son

and make a nice impression on your mom. Even if I haven't agreed to participate in the book, I want to show your family that I can be as hospitable as my dad."

"And us staying with you is the only way you can do that?"

"No, but it would make it easier."

"What if my mom figures out that you and I…"

"Is that what you're worried about?" He tried to reassure her. "We'll be as careful as possible. I promise that we won't take any chances that we shouldn't take."

"Okay." She came over to him. "I'll accept your invitation. And I'll tell my mom that you want the opportunity to entertain her and Chance the way Kirby will be entertaining them at his house."

"Thanks. That'd be great." A new idea sprang into his head. "You know what I should do to get the hospitality ball rolling? Get everyone together for a barbecue. I can invite my mom and Lester over when your mom and Chance are here."

"I like that," she readily replied. "It would be nice for our families to get acquainted."

"I think so, too." He reached for her, taking her in his arms. "We're not going to let anyone know that we're sleeping together, but we can certainly show them what good friends we are." He nuzzled her hair. "Exactly how long do we have until your mom and Chance get here?"

She looked up at him. "Three days."

"Then let's get our stuff moved in as soon as we

can." He thought about how he'd poked around in her kitchen earlier. "We'll have to empty out your fridge and bring your food here, too. But we can also go into town for groceries."

"How about if I make dinner for you tonight?"

"That sounds great." He would never turn down a home-cooked meal. "You can fix anything you want."

"Spaghetti and meatballs is my specialty, but you have to help."

"I'd be glad to." He wanted to spend as much time with her as possible, in whatever ways he could.

Libby inhaled the aroma of spices. She'd already made a big batch of meatballs that were simmering in a pot of dark, rich sauce.

She put the water on to boil for the pasta and sprinkled in a generous helping of salt. She didn't add oil because all it did was make the noodles greasy, preventing the sauce from sticking to them later. She'd learned that from Becker's grandma. Nonna, as he called her.

She glanced at Matt. She'd put him in charge of the salad, and just for the fun of it she'd taught him how to curl cucumbers and make radishes look like roses. That was more know-how she'd learned from Nonna.

"I miss doing things like this," she said.

He glanced up at her from where he stood at the center island, creating his masterpiece. "Things like what?" He smiled, then winked. "Having affairs? And here I thought I was your first."

"Ha ha." She rolled her eyes. "I was talking about cooking with—" *Oh, my God*, she thought. She'd almost said *my husband*. She recovered quickly and said, "My man."

But that didn't sound much better. The only man she'd ever had besides Matt *was* her husband.

He stilled his knife, gazing at the vegetables in front of him. "Did you and Becker make this exact meal together?"

"Sometimes we did." By now, her hands were shaking. She couldn't believe she'd nearly referred to Matt as her husband. What part of her brain had conjured up that crazy notion? "Becker was part Italian. This is his maternal grandma's recipe."

Matt's shoulders tensed. "So you chose the same dish for me?"

"I wasn't thinking of how it would affect you." Or how it would affect her, either. "It's just something I wanted to make for you."

"I'm sorry. I didn't mean to cause a fuss. Maybe it's just that Becker is still a bit of a mystery to me."

Her hands hadn't quit shaking. She brushed them against her skirt, using the fabric like an apron. "I've told you lots of things about him."

"You never said what he did for a living. You never said where he's buried, either."

"Becker doesn't have a grave." Her heart squeezed inside her chest. Deciding what to do with his remains had been a painful experience. "He was cremated."

"Did you sprinkle his ashes somewhere special?"

"No." She doubted that anyone other than Matt would be asking her these types of questions. But given his history with Sandy, he probably couldn't help himself. "Becker's ashes are in a gold-and-green urn at my apartment. I chose gold because of the plain gold wedding band I gave him and green because of how environmentally conscious he was. He worked for a company that produced wind turbines and solar panels. He thought of it as an earth-friendly job."

"That's nice that he respected Mother Earth. That he was such a caring guy."

"In the beginning, I thought about getting a permit to sprinkle his ashes at the beach or in the mountains. But I changed my mind. Once I brought his remains home, I took comfort in having them there." She'd realized that she needed a connection to Becker. And so did Chance. Her son had his own sweet and loving concept of death.

Matt watched her, as intense as ever. "I knew you were still grieving."

"Not in the way you think I am."

"But you're still hurting, Libby."

"Of course I am. I lost the man I loved, the father of my child. But I don't need to dwell on it every moment of the day." To stop herself from crying, she took a long, grueling breath, letting it rattle her lungs. "I'm still here, and he isn't. I have to go on with my life, wherever that life takes me."

"For now, it brought you to me."

For now. The temporary sound of those words delivered another threat of tears to her eyes. And the last thing she wanted was to bawl in front of Matt.

Anxious, she returned to cooking. It was time to put the spaghetti in the pot. Time to focus. To have a normal affair.

"I'd like to make a deal with you," she said.

He remained at the center island, the salad half made. "What kind of deal?"

"That neither of us falls in love."

He flinched, looking uncomfortably confused. Then he asked, "In the future, like with other people? Or did you mean with each other?"

"With each other." She couldn't handle falling in love with him, and then being in California while he was in Texas and longing for the comfort of his big, strong body next to hers. Nor could she bear to mistake him for her husband, tripping up like that again, putting him in Becker's place. "I just want it to be free and easy."

"That's what I want, too. Loving you would hurt too much, Libby. It would be too much like what happened with Sandy. I've already been stressing about you being a widow."

"Then we're in agreement. We're not going to get more attached than we should."

"Absolutely." He waggled his eyebrows. "We'll just be friends with benefits."

He sauntered over to her and fed her a slice of red bell pepper he'd chopped. She chewed and swallowed, and he said, "I should do you right here."

"Against the stove? With the spaghetti boiling and the meatballs simmering? We'd burn our butts off."

He grinned. "You're right. There's already plenty of steam in here. I'll have to get you after dinner."

"And I'll have to hold you to it."

He angled his head. "Did we just make another deal?"

"So it seems." A sex deal. A no-love deal. They were on a roll. She quickly kissed him and went back to fixing the meal, content with both of the deals they'd made.

Matt sat across from Libby at the dining room table, twining spaghetti around his fork. She sipped her wine, and he watched the ladylike way she curled her fingers around the stem of the glass. He didn't want to fall in love with Libby any more than she wanted to fall for him. And now that she'd brought it up, he felt an overwhelming sense of relief.

He had to give her credit for getting it out in the open. Maybe if he'd done that with Sandy up front, he would have been more cautious about getting involved with her. Maybe he wouldn't have even married her at all. But he didn't have to worry about developing something with Libby that was going to blow up in his face. She'd eliminated the prospect of getting too attached.

So far, he and Libby had only known each other for two weeks. And in another two weeks, she would be leaving for good. To most people, that would seem like nothing. But he'd fallen for Sandy within that amount of time. Things sometimes happened fast. Apparently Libby knew that, too, taking into account how quickly she and Becker had gotten together.

"I'm glad we figured things out," he said.

"So am I. And look at this fabulous dinner we created."

"I didn't do all that much."

"Are you kidding?" She skewered a radish and held it up in the light from the chandelier. "Look at this work of art."

"Me and my trusty knife. Who knew I could do something like that?" He lingered over his spaghetti, pondering his affection for her. He thought about their friendship. Their sexual chemistry. He liked knowing their affair was going to end without hurting more than it should.

She ate the radish. "You know what I just realized? We forgot about dessert for tonight."

"No, we didn't. Or I didn't, anyway. I got a carton of spumoni when we were at the store. You must have been in another aisle when I tossed it into the cart."

"Thanks for thinking of it. Italian ice cream is just what we need to go with this."

"I'm good at remembering the sweet stuff." He flirted with her. "I like sweet women, too."

She flicked a drop of her wine at him, missing him by a mile. "I hope I'm sweet enough for you."

"You definitely are. But you have terrible aim." He flicked his wine at her, hitting his mark.

She laughed, and they finished their main course. When it was time for dessert, they cleared their plates and went into the kitchen together. He took the spumoni out of the freezer and tasted it directly from the carton.

"Matt," she scolded him. "Don't I get some?"

"Of course you do." He gave her the next bite, feeding it to her. "What do you think?"

She sucked it off the spoon. "It's yummy."

He agreed. But not as yummy as what he intended to do to her. He dropped a dollop of the ice cream down the front of her blouse.

"Oh, my God!" She jumped and shivered. "That's cold."

"Sorry. My bad. You better take off your top and let me clean you up."

"You did that on purpose." She removed her blouse, slanting him a wanton look. The spumoni was now dripping into her bra. "Maybe I should take this off, too?"

"Yeah, I think you should. Or maybe you should let me do it." He unfastened the hooks, and without the slightest delay, he licked the dessert off her breasts. He swirled his tongue back and forth, over each pert pink nipple.

She moaned and pulled him closer. "You really are going to do me in the kitchen."

"Damn right, I am." He had a condom in his pocket; he'd put it there earlier for just such an occasion. He was going to carry one everywhere. Or everywhere that Libby would be.

They slid to the floor, and he reached under her skirt and pulled off her panties. But he didn't remove her skirt. He merely bunched it around her hips.

She opened her legs, and he slid between them and yanked his jeans down. He left the spumoni on the counter. But he wasn't worried about it melting. He intended for this to happen fast. Hard and fast, he thought.

He sheathed himself with the condom and slammed into her, making her gasp from the quick, rough invasion. While he moved deep inside, she fisted his T-shirt, clawing at the material as if it was his skin.

She muttered something deliciously dirty in his ear, and he turned his head and captured her mouth. They mated like animals, rolling all over the floor, the limestone cool against their bodies. Hot sex on a cold surface. It didn't get any freer than that.

He aroused every warm, wet part of her, and she begged him for more. And he gave her everything he could. Libby with the stunning blue eyes, he thought, with the tangled blond hair.

He kissed her again, and she came in a flurry of gyrating thrusts and shaky moans, dragging him into a nail-biting, pelvis-rocking, brain-numbing climax of his own.

Minutes ticked by when neither them could find the strength to move. Finally, he got up, ditched the condom and zipped his pants. When he returned, she was still sprawled out on the floor, topless, with her skirt askew.

"Let me help you." He offered a hand, and she smiled and latched onto him.

Matt grabbed the spumoni and two spoons, and she fished around for her blouse. Locating it near the dishwasher, she put it on, leaving it unbuttoned. Her bra was forgotten.

From there, he took her to his room, where they sat on the bed and dug into the ice cream, enjoying the nighttime coziness of being lovers.

Nine

After three wondrous days, Libby's sexy stint of sleeping in the master suite with Matt was over. Her mom and Chance would be here this afternoon.

She turned toward Matt. He stood beside an oak armoire, looking as solid and rugged as the furniture. They were in the guest room where she would be staying.

"You seem nervous," he said.

"I'm starting to get worried again that my mom might figure us out."

"We're going to be careful, Libby."

"I know." She glanced at the bed and its sunburst-patterned quilt. It was a lovely room, with all sorts of creature comforts. But she was going to miss sleeping with Matt. She gestured to the adjoining bath. "I staged the bathroom so it looks like I got ready there this morning. I left my toothbrush and toothpaste out. I lined up my fragrances on the counter, too, and left the cap off the perfume I used today."

He came toward her and sniffed her skin. "Do you really think your mom is going to notice something like that?"

"I'm just trying to be thorough."

He jumped onto the bed and pulled her down with him. "I think you're being paranoid."

She squealed when he yanked up her T-shirt and tickled her ribs. She laughed and tried to push him away. "We're making a disaster out of this bed."

"So it'll look like you did a crappy job of making it this morning."

"Are you sure it's not going to look like some big, sexy cowboy ravished me on it?"

"I'm not ravishing you. But I can if you want me to."

"You need to behave." He'd already done a bang-up job of ravishing her every night since she'd moved in with him. He'd had his way with her this morning, too, hauling her into the shower with him. Shower sex had become their thing. Along with kitchen floor sex. And every other kind of sex they could think of.

To keep the tickling at bay, she whopped him with a pillow. He wrestled the pillow away, set it aside and kissed her, soft and slow, his lips tender against hers. But that was as far as it went: a warm, romantic kiss.

She got up and righted her T-shirt. He was still reclining on the bed. She wanted to slip back into his arms, but she refrained. She needed to control her urges for him.

"I'm really glad I'm going to meet your son," he said.

His interest in Chance made her heart beat faster. She had a soft spot when it came to her child. "He's a chatterbox, so don't be surprised if he talks your ear off."

"That's okay." He smiled at her for a breathless moment and climbed off the bed. "His mama talks my ear off sometimes, too."

"I do not." She fluffed the pillow that she'd used to smack him, and together they smoothed the quilt, him on one side, her on the other.

"I'm just trying to lighten your mood."

"I know." Her nerves remained on edge. Libby wasn't used to hiding things from her family. She'd dated Becker openly before she married him. But that was different than what she was doing with Matt. "I just have a lot on my mind."

Matt went quiet. Then he said, "I hope Chance likes the room I chose for him. When the twins were here, I offered each of them their own room, but they wanted to stay together. They were inseparable that way. They brought their bunk beds with them. But all of that is gone now."

"Chance has bunk beds in his room, for when a friend or cousin spends the night. Children that age enjoy pairing up."

"What's your apartment like?" Curiosity colored his voice. There was a searching look in his eyes, too.

"We're on the first floor of a triplex. It's not walkable to the beach, but there's a bus we can take."

"Can't you drive to the beach?"

"Yes, but parking is a nightmare." She thought about how modest her place was. "Becker and I were hoping to buy a house someday, but it wasn't in our budget."

"What about the book advance? Can you use it as a down payment on a condo or something?"

"I wish I could, but property is ridiculously expensive in my area, and I need to live on the advance. For now, that's my only income. I used to supplement my writing with temp jobs. Hopefully I'll get more book deals in the future and won't have to do that again."

"I'm sure you will. You're one of the most ambitious women I've ever known. But you're sweet and homey, too."

"Thank you." That meant a lot coming from him. "I'm doing what I can to be a single mom and have a successful career, too."

"I hope you're able to have your own house someday. At the beach or wherever you want it to be."

For a heart-jarring second, she envisioned living here with him. Clearly, she was losing her marbles; those little suckers were rolling right out of her head. The other day she'd laid down the law about not falling in love, and today she was having cozy thoughts about moving in with him?

Libby needed to get a hold of her emotions, a tight, tight hold on them, especially before Chance and her mom got here.

Chance Mitchell Penn was a whirlwind, a fast-talking, toy-slinging tyke with bright blue eyes. It was only the first day, and he was following Matt all over the house, yapping up a storm. Right off the bat, Matt learned that Chance hated shampooing his hair. In fact, he wore it in a buzz cut to make washing it easier. He didn't like taking baths, either, or going to bed early.

Libby's son had an opinion on everything: steamed vegetables were gross, but raw ones were fun and snappy; girls acted silly when they giggled with their friends, and boys acted stupid when they got into fights. Matt had never been so amused. He adored this kid already. Of course he was trying to keep it in perspective and not get too attached, the way he'd done with the twins when he'd first met them. But damn, Chance was tough to resist.

Libby's mother, Debra, was far more reserved. She didn't run off at the mouth like Chance. Nor did she dress in flashy clothes like Libby. Although her hair was blond, she sported a short, simple, conservative do. But in spite of their differences, the love between mother and daughter was apparent. He suspected that Libby's father was a decent guy, too. She'd been raised in a normal household. No country star dad or mistress mom.

Not that Matt was blaming his mother. He loved

her as much as Libby obviously loved her mom. But he'd always longed for the kind of family Libby had.

"Can I see my room again?" Chance asked Matt.

"If you want to." Matt had already showed it to him twice, but maybe three times would be the charm.

The boy bounced on his heels. "You come, too, Mom." He grabbed Libby's hand, then glanced over at his grandmother, who was seated in a living room recliner, reading the ranch brochure. "You can stay there, Nana."

Debra glanced up. "Why, thanks for that."

"No prob'em," Chance said.

Matt caught Debra's eye, and she sent him a vacation-weary smile. She looked ready for a nap. Traveling with a rambunctious six-year-old had obviously worn her out. But at least Chance was astute enough to know when his grandmother was tired and needed a break.

Chance's room offered a queen-size bed and a pic-ture window with a view of the hills. It also had a big flat-screen TV. All the guest rooms did. Earlier Libby had set the parental controls, which had given Matt a familiar feeling. When the twins first moved in, Sandy had done that, as well.

"This is cool," Chance said. "Can I jump on the bed?"

Matt started to say *why not?* but Libby cut him off and said, "Get real," to her son. That obviously meant no.

The boy shrugged and shifted his feet, rocking back and forth. He'd yet to be still. He gazed up at the ceil-ing. A second later, he asked Matt, "Did you know my dad is in heaven?"

More déjà vu. The twins used to talk about how their daddy was in heaven, too. "Yes, your mother told me."

Chance kept rocking. "He's in an angel pot at our house."

Matt assumed he was referring to the urn that contained Becker's ashes. He dared a glance at Libby. But she was looking at her son.

"He flies around at night and watches over us," Chance said. "That's what angels who live in pots do. They're sort of like genies, only they don't give you wishes. But if they did, I would wish for my dad to be here with me."

Matt nodded as if he understood. And in his own mixed-up way, he did. He'd lived through something like this before. But as similar as it seemed, it wasn't exactly the same. He wasn't repeating the mistakes he'd made with Sandy. He wasn't going to fall in love with Libby or marry her or compete with her late husband's memory.

"Wanna see some pictures of my dad?" Chance asked.

"Sure. I'd like to see your father." Matt wasn't going to deny the boy.

"Okay, but he wasn't an angel back then. He was just a person. People don't become angels till they go to heaven." Chance nudged Libby. "Go get your phone so I can show him the pictures."

She put a hand on her son's shoulder, but her gaze

was on Matt. She smiled, oh so softly, at him. A thank-you, he thought, for indulging her child.

She left the room, and Chance glanced at the bed, as if he was considering jumping on it while she was gone. Or maybe he was just planning on doing that later, when no one was around.

Libby returned, and the three of them sat on the edge of the bed, with Chance in the middle. As he scrolled through the photographs, he narrated each one. He moved quickly; it was clear that he had them memorized.

Becker was smiling in every picture. He had a happy, relaxed air about him, with a tanned complexion, a neatly trimmed goatee and hair that was long on top and clipped close on the sides, the same medium-brown shade as his son's.

"You look like your dad," Matt said to Chance. They had comparable features, except for the eyes. Those had definitely come from Libby.

"Check this out." Chance stopped at a wedding photo of his parents. "See how big my mom's belly is? That's me in there."

Matt studied the picture. Libby looked young and beautiful, a pregnant bride in her sparkling white gown and spiffy white boots.

He leaned over and said to her, "That's how I imagined you when you described your wedding to me."

"It was the happiest day of my life." She put her arm around Chance. "Along with the day he was born."

Chance scrolled to another photo, an image of his

father holding him on his lap. Becker was grinning like a loon.

Libby said, "That's the last picture that was taken of them together."

Matt didn't know how to respond. Even chatty Chance had gone quiet. By now, he could feel the boy staring at him.

Then the kid asked, "Are you a real cowboy?"

The change of topic threw Matt off-kilter. He was still looking at the last-ever picture of Chance and his dad.

"I told you he was," Libby said, chiming in with an answer.

"Yeah, but is he a *real* one?"

"Darned right, I am," Matt said. "When I was your age, I was competing in junior rodeos."

Chance's mouth dropped open. "You were doing that when you were small, like me?"

"I used to ride and rope my little butt off." Matt remembered the joy it gave him in those early years. Without it, he would have been lost. "My mom took me to my events."

Chance was still slack-jawed in wonder. "She must be a great mom."

"Yeah, she is." Not a conventional one, but a great one. "She lives here on the ranch with her husband. They're going to come by later in the week for a barbecue."

The kid looked over at Libby. "Can I learn to become a rodeo cowboy?"

She ran her hand over his buzz cut. "How about if you just pretend to be one for now?"

"That's not the same as doing it." He frowned at the phone in his hand. Somewhere in the midst of their conversation, the screen had gone black. He touched it, bringing the picture of him and Becker back up. "I bet my dad would let me do it if he was here."

Libby sighed. She seemed sad and alone, as widowed as a woman could be. Particularly when she said, "I take you on pony rides at the big park in LA."

Chance pouted. "That's baby stuff."

Matt wondered if he should come to the rescue. Not as a father figure, he warned himself, but as a cowboy.

When he thought Chance might cry, he stepped in and said, "Sometimes I give roping lessons on the ranch. And if it's okay with your mom, I can teach you a few pointers. But we'd be doing it on the ground, not on horseback. That's how everyone learns at first."

"That would be so much fun." Libby's son danced in his seat. "Is it okay, Mom? Is it?"

She nodded, and Chance leaped into her arms and hugged her. After they separated, he grinned at Matt and handed him the phone, tearing off out of the room to tell his grandmother the good news.

Matt and Libby both fell silent. During the gentle pause, Matt returned the phone to her, and she pressed it against her chest. The picture of Becker and Chance was still on the screen.

"I wish I could kiss you for what you did for my son," she said in a whisper.

He wanted to kiss her, too. But he couldn't. Not here. Not like this. He spoke as softly as she did. "Was it your idea to tell him that his dad lived in an angel pot?"

"I told him that the urn was connected to his father and his dad was in heaven, but he came up with the rest of it. I never said that Becker was an angel flying around our house at night. Nor did I mention genies or wishes that couldn't be granted. Becker's family didn't encourage those stories, either." She lowered the phone to her lap. "It's just Chance's way of comforting himself, of rationalizing why his dad can't come back to us."

"I'm sorry he doesn't have a father anymore." Matt couldn't think of anything else to say, except to give his condolences. No child should lose his or her parent.

"He doesn't have many memories of Becker, but he tries to create them. He loves showing off those pictures. But it doesn't always help." Libby tucked a strand of hair behind her ear, where it curled toward her cheek. "I can't thank you enough for offering to teach him to rope. You're already becoming his hero."

A lump formed in his throat. "He's a nice kid."

"And you're a really nice man."

"I just did what I thought was right." He tried to play it down, but with the tender way she was looking at him, he was actually starting to feel like her son's hero.

If only for a little while.

* * *

On the day of the family barbecue, Libby analyzed the people gathered around the table. You'd think that Julie and her mom had known each other for years. They hit it off beautifully. Lester was his usual kind self, and Chance was chomping on his burger and smiling at Matt. Chance had loved every moment of his first week on the ranch, and most of his joy had come from spending time with Matt.

As promised, Matt had been teaching him how to rope. The dummy they used—a plastic steer head attached to a bale of straw—was out on the grass. By now, Libby had gotten used to seeing it. Chance had even named it Stanley, short for Stanley the Steer. As for the rest of Chance's gear, Matt had provided him with an extrasoft, kid-sized rope and one cotton glove.

Libby was downright crazy about Matt, especially after seeing how amazing he was with her son, but she was being careful not to let her attraction to him show. So far she'd lucked out with her mom. They'd been keeping Chance and her so busy attending group activities on the ranch, she didn't have time to notice the heat between Libby and Matt.

Matt's mom didn't seem to be aware of it, either. Just yesterday, Libby had interviewed Julie for the book. So in that regard, Libby's work on the ranch was done. Unless Matt miraculously changed his mind and agreed to be interviewed. But that wasn't very likely.

Chance wiggled in his seat, drawing Libby's attention to him. After swallowing the big, messy bite in his mouth, he said to her, "You should have Matt teach you to rope. You'd be good at it. Not as good as I am," he added, being young and boastful, "but still good."

"That's okay. I'd rather watch you." She'd seen how close Matt got to Chance during their lessons. She didn't need Matt getting that close to her, at least not in public. Unfortunately, they weren't doing it in private, either. It wasn't easy to slip off together. In fact, it was proving impossible. They hadn't kissed or touched or done anything even remotely romantic the entire week.

"Come on, Mom. Just try it."

Libby blew out her breath. Chance could be a pest when he wanted something, and at the moment he wanted her to be a roper. She decided that her best line of defense was to change the subject. "How about if you just finish your burger, and let me eat mine?"

Chance rolled his eyes. Just then, Matt turned his gaze on Libby. Apparently he'd been listening to the exchange.

"Don't you want to be a cowgirl?" he asked.

She almost kicked him under the table. He knew darned well that she'd already ridden him like a cowgirl, buck naked on his lap. Surely that counted for something.

"She's probably just scared of Stanley," Chance said.

Great. Her son was back in the game, baiting her.

"That steer head is pretty scary." This came from Libby's mother. *Her mother*. Good grief. So now she was joining in on it, too?

The conversation sparked Julie's interest, as well.

She said, "I always thought the ones with the red eyes were a little creepy. But Matt liked them when he was a kid. He thought they looked more menacing."

Libby gazed across the grass at Stanley. Its plastic eyes glowed in the sunlight, glaring at her like balls of fire. Its horns were rather demonic, too. "I'm not scared of the stupid steer head."

Matt's tone was blasé. "It sort of sounds as if you are."

Lester chuckled under his breath before stuffing his face with another spoonful of potato salad.

"This is a conspiracy," Libby said.

"It's just a roping lesson." Matt took a slice of watermelon and put it on his plate. He'd already eaten two burgers and a bacon-wrapped hot dog smothered in cheese. Sometimes that man had an enormous appetite. And not just for food. She knew his hunger all too well.

"Just do it, Mom." Chance refused to let up. "I'll even help you."

"All right. Fine." She gave in. The bigger the stink she made, the worse it was going to get. "When we're done eating, you and Matt can teach me to become a cowgirl." She shot a glance at Matt, and he smiled a bit too triumphantly.

When everyone finished their food, Julie helped Libby's mom clear the table, leaving Libby and Matt free for the lesson. Lester wandered off to have a smoke, and Chance hopped along with Libby and Matt, bouncing like a kangaroo.

"First things first." Matt gave Chance his hat. "Will you hold on to this for me?"

"Sure." The boy plopped it on his own head.

It was too big for him, but he wore it proudly, reminding Libby of the oversize hat Matt had worn in the childhood picture she'd seen of him at his mom's house.

"I'll be back." Matt went into a shed and came back with an adult-sized rope and a glove.

He gave Libby the glove. "This should fit you."

She put it on her right hand.

Her son piped up. "In team roping, the first guy ropes the horns, and he's called a header. The other guy ropes the heels, and he's called a heeler."

Libby knew all of that. Her obsession with cowboys had come from watching rodeos on TV.

Chance adjusted the hat, which kept falling forward on his head. "Matt is a header. That's what he's teaching me to be, too. It's okay for women to be team ropers and to play against the men."

Libby knew that, too. But at the moment, she was more concerned about swooning over her lover than competing with him.

Matt said, "First, I'm going to show you how to a coil a rope." He tossed the rope and demonstrated, explaining each step.

She watched him, listening to him the best she could.

He stood next to her and threw the rope again. "Now you try."

She did her best. But it wasn't quite right. Matt covered her hand with his and showed her again. "See?" he said. "Like this."

Yes, she saw. She felt the warmth of his touch, too.

If he turned her face toward his, she could kiss him, which was the worst thought she could've had. Chance was watching.

"You're doing good, Mom," he said.

No, she wasn't. But she thanked her son, anyway. She certainly wouldn't be roping a steer anytime soon, not even Stanley, with its red, raging eyes. Libby could barely breathe, let alone coil the rope. How in the world was she going to graduate to the next step?

But somehow, she did. Matt moved her along, giving her an accelerated lesson. By then, Julie, Lester and her mom were back on the patio. Libby felt like an animal in a zoo, with everyone watching. Matt was showing her how to build a loop with the rope.

"I did great at this part," Chance said.

Libby sucked at it. "I can't learn this in a day."

Matt brushed up against her, as if it was part of the lesson. Or maybe it was. She couldn't tell anymore.

"We're just doing this for fun," he said.

Her idea of fun would be slipping into his room tonight. Not standing here with an audience, getting weak in the knees.

"Let me take over," Chance said, eager to show off what he knew. He returned Matt's hat, then put on his glove and picked up his rope.

Libby stood back, but not far enough, apparently.

Matt reached for her hand and tugged her farther back, making sure that Chance didn't accidentally hit her with the rope. But Libby already felt as if she'd been struck upside the head, wishing she really could slip into Matt's room tonight.

And let him lasso her to the bed.

Ten

At 1:00 a.m. Libby was awake, thinking about Matt. But she wasn't going to go sneaking into his room. She wouldn't dare risk something like that, not while she was under the same roof as Chance and her mother.

Nonetheless, she switched on the lamp next to her bed. Being in the dark, fretting under the covers, certainly wasn't helping. She could turn on the TV, she supposed. Since sleep eluded her, she needed something to keep her mind occupied.

Just as she reached for the remote, a knock sounded on her door. She jumped out of bed. Was it Chance? No, that didn't make sense. What would he be doing up at this hour? Besides, he wouldn't knock. If he needed her for some reason, he would march right in, bellowing, "Mom!"

Her mother, then? She had no idea why her mom would be awake, either, and coming to see her.

A sudden panic set in. Was it Matt? Was he—

"Libby?" he said from the other side.

Okay, so it was Matt. But dang it, he should know better than to come to her room at this hour. Already the thought of being with him was making her heart pound.

She went to the door, opened it a crack and gazed out at him. He looked as if he'd gotten dressed in a hurry, with no belt, no hat and a T-shirt hanging loose. His midnight-black hair was barely combed.

"What's going on?" she asked.

"My birthing attendant just called. We've got a mare that's getting ready to foal."

"Right now?"

He nodded. "They tend to foal in the middle of the night. Anyway, I noticed that your light was on and I wondered if you wanted to go to the broodmare barn with me." He smiled like a nervous new dad. "I always assist with the births."

She opened the door wider. "I'd love to go with you. I've never seen a mare foal." Human babies tended to arrive in the middle of the night, too. Or Chance did, anyway.

"The labor comes in stages. She's already in the first stage. Once her water breaks, it'll be the second stage and that's when the foal will emerge. The third one is the expulsion of the placenta. But her water is probably going to break anytime now."

"I'll throw myself together and meet you in the living room. I need to write a note, too, to my mom, in case she or Chance wakes up and I'm not here. I doubt they will, but it will make me feel better to do it." She hurriedly asked, "How long do you think we'll be gone?"

"I don't know. It could last until daylight. But more than likely, we'll be back before then."

"I'll tell her it could take all night. Then if she's up before we get back, she won't worry."

"Okay. I'll see you in a few."

He turned and walked away, leaving her with an excited feeling. She rushed to peel off her nightgown and climb into a pair of jeans and an oversize blouse. She didn't have time to fuss with a bra, so she skipped it. No makeup and tousled hair would also have to do. This wasn't a glamour gig.

She dug around in the closet and reached for the nearest boots. She grabbed a jacket and her phone, too.

Next, she scribbled out the note to her mom and headed for the living room. On the way, she put the note on the kitchen table, where it would be most visible.

"Ready?" Matt asked as she approached him.

She nodded. She was good to go.

They climbed in his truck, and he started the engine. He backed out of the driveway and tore off down the private road that led to and from his house.

"Earlier, when I knocked on your door, I noticed your light was already on," he said, repeating what he'd told her when he'd first come to her room. "So what kept you up tonight?" he asked.

"You," she answered honestly. "We haven't been together at all this week."

"I know." He adjusted his hands on the wheel. "It's been making me crazy. I've spent some sleepless nights, too, wondering how we can be alone."

She sent him a goofy grin. "We're alone now."

"Yeah, on our way to birthing a foal." He rewarded her with a foolish grin in return. "If you want, I can send the attendant home after the foal arrives, and if there's time left over, you and I can stay there by ourselves until the sun comes up."

Her pulse spiked. "There won't be any ranch hands around between now and then?"

"No. It'll be just us."

This outing was starting to sound beautifully romantic. So much so, she got a dreamy pang in the center of her stomach. "I hope there's time left over."

"Me, too. We can celebrate with some sparkling cider. When I was a kid, my mom and I did that whenever we had a new foal. I always keep a supply on hand now."

"That's a nice tradition." She was eager to have this experience with him. "We'll have to bring Chance and my mom back later to see the foal."

"Definitely. My mom and Lester, too. They're always happy to have new life around here."

"Who wouldn't be?" She remembered the joy of seeing Chance for the first time. She recalled the long and grueling labor, too. "Why do mares typically foal at night?" she asked.

"They like to feel secure, when there's less activity around them. They can even prolong their labor if they aren't comfortable in their surroundings."

When Libby and Matt arrived at the broodmare barn, it was quiet, giving the mare the security she needed. The attendant, Hector Ramirez, was an older man with lots of experience. The mare, a lovely sorrel quarter horse with a flaxen mane, was known as Annie Oakley.

Annie's timing was spot on. Her water broke soon after Matt and Libby got there. Fascinated, Libby stood on the other side of the stall and watched.

An amniotic sac appeared with the foal inside it. Matt checked to make sure the foal was in the correct position. Apparently it was, with its front feet first and its soles pointing down.

The foal's nose and knees came next. Or that was how it looked to Libby; she couldn't quite tell because of how it was curled up. Annie rested before the shoulders appeared. Then she finished pushing, until the whole body was free of the birth canal.

The damp foal broke through the water bag and was as adorable as could be. Matt cleared the membrane from its nostrils. Libby smiled. Annie was the proud parent of a perfect little filly.

The passing of the placenta took about an hour.

Hector checked to make sure there were no pieces missing, except for the hole where the foal had been.

Neither Matt nor Hector cut the umbilical cord. It happened naturally, when the mare stood to examine her baby. The tenderness between Annie and the foal gave Libby the sweet and unsettling urge to have another child. She glanced over at Matt and imagined having her next baby with him.

Seriously?

She squeezed her eyes shut, trying to block the insanity spiraling through her mind. But it wasn't helping. The thought of having a baby with him wouldn't go away.

Matt and Hector exited the stall and headed to the restroom to clean up. Libby stayed where she was, panicking inside.

The men returned, and Matt dismissed Hector. The entire process had gone quickly and efficiently, with plenty of time to spare for Matt and Libby to be alone. After Hector left the barn, Matt came up behind Libby.

"Look," he said. "The foal is standing. She should start nursing soon, too. We need to stay nearby to make sure she eats. Then we can take a break and spend some time together."

She gazed at the little beauty, wobbling on its spindly legs. Having a baby with Matt was out of the question. Yet the thought kept invading her mind.

Matt slipped his arms around Libby's waist, bringing the back of her body closer to his front. She was glad that he was behind her, giving her time to compose herself. By now, her legs were starting to wobble, worse than the foal's.

Once the filly began taking her first meal, Matt quietly asked, "Did you nurse Chance or was he bottle-fed?"

"I nursed him." But this wasn't a topic she wanted to discuss. It just made her want another baby even more. With Matt, she thought. With a man she vowed *not* to love.

"It's cute how the foal is getting the milk on her whiskers," he said. "I really love being part of this."

"You're going to make a great dad someday." It was a stupid thing to say, especially with the way she was feeling.

"I hope so." He released his hold on her. "We can have the cider now, if you want."

"I'd like that." Her mouth had gone terribly dry.

"Then I'll go get it." He gestured to another section of the barn. "There's an empty stall with fresh straw. You can wait over there. I'll get a blanket for us, too."

While he headed to a supply room, she entered the stall and prayed that her knees wouldn't buckle. Was it possible that she was falling in love with Matt, doing exactly what she wasn't supposed to do? Of course it was possible, she told herself.

Why else would she be feeling this way? She wanted to roll up and die over the ache she knew it was going to cause. How was she going to leave the ranch, loving him, longing for him, missing him beyond reason?

He returned with a big plaid blanket, a bottle of

cider and two plastic champagne flutes. He spread the blanket on the straw, and Libby sat down and removed her jacket. She wasn't the least bit relaxed, but she pretended to be.

He joined her on the blanket, opened the bottle and poured their drinks. He tapped his glass to hers and said, "Here's to the new filly on the Flying Creek Ranch."

"What are you going to name her?"

"I don't know. Maybe Chance can help me come up with something."

"That will thrill him, I'm sure." She sipped the cider, grateful for its crisp apple flavor. The carbonation was helping a bit, too. She needed it to settle the jumpiness in her stomach. "He's been having the time of his life here." Not only was Matt teaching her son to rope, they'd been taking Chance out on trail rides with a gentle old mare that Matt had chosen for him to ride. Was it any wonder she was falling in love with Matt? Her son adored him, too.

He drained his glass and refilled it. "I'm impressed with what a fine cowboy Chance is turning out to be. If you're able to keep the riding and roping lessons up, he's really going to improve."

"I'll look into a trainer in my area." She wanted to give Chance the opportunity to grow into whatever he wanted to be. But it pained her to think that Matt wasn't going to part of his future. Or hers. Libby's life was going to seem empty without Matt. So horribly empty. If she could make her feelings for him go away, she would. But it was too late for that. The damage had already been done.

"I can ask around for recommendations for trainers. Offhand, I don't know anyone in Los Angeles, but I'd be glad to check into it."

"Thank you. That would be helpful." She drank more of her cider and commented on their surroundings. "It's so quiet here now, with just the two of us."

He moved closer. "It's nice. This affair of ours."

Their free-and-easy affair, she thought, mocking herself for coming up with that. She'd already lost her husband, and now she was falling for someone who didn't belong to her. It didn't get more complicated than that.

When he leaned into her, she reached for him, desperate for a kiss. Even as emotionally tormented as she was, she couldn't deny the need to be with him.

Their mouths came together, the sensation passionately familiar. In between kisses, he unbuttoned her blouse, and she lifted his T-shirt over his head.

They stood and undressed all the way, draping their clothes over the stall door, making it seem like a bedroom. The nighttime lights in the barn enhanced the ambience.

He lowered her to the blanket, using it as a bed. The straw beneath it was bumpy, but somehow warm and inviting, too. Everything seemed right yet wrong. Good yet bad. Libby wished that she'd never fallen in love with him. It would be so much easier if she could have left things the way they were. But to him, nothing had changed. He didn't know how she was feeling, and she wasn't going to tell him.

She noticed that her glass had tipped over, her cider spilling onto a corner of the blanket. Matt's glass was still upright.

"What are you looking at?" he asked.

"How my glass fell over but yours didn't."

"Maybe I'm just more careful than you are."

He definitely was, she thought. Not just with his cider, but with his heart. "I'd rather see yours spilled, too. I don't want you to be the only careful one."

"Whatever you say." He flung out his arm and knocked over his flute, sending cider pouring out of it. "Is that better?"

She nodded and pulled him down on top of her, biting and kissing and clawing, making marks on his skin. She wanted to brand him, to make him hers, if only for tonight.

"This might be our last time together," she said, trying to explain her frantic behavior. "We might not find the time to be alone again."

"I know." He pushed back against the pressure. "I'll do whatever you want, however you want it."

"Then do it fast." She wanted it quick and hard, to crash and burn, to shatter from the ache of loving him.

He used his fingers to stimulate her. He put his mouth on her, too, inciting slick, wet heat. She reacted to every sexy thing he did, arching her body, mewling and moaning.

When he put on protection and entered her, she

knew there was no way out. No matter what pace he set, her heart spun like a battered pinwheel.

His stomach muscles tensed with every thrust. Immersed in the motion, she skimmed a hand down his abs. She lowered her fingers, dangerously close to where they were joined.

She kissed him, savoring the taste of his lips. He took her arms and lifted them above her head, pinning her in place. Libby gulped her next breath. She always got excited when he did that.

"Are you close?" he asked, his penetration strong and deep.

"Yes." She needed a release, to let it rush through her body.

Sweat beaded on his forehead. He was close, too. She knew he liked for them to come at the same time. She wanted to give him what he wanted. She longed to give him everything, even what he didn't want. Love, she thought.

Damnable love.

If only he could see the secret in her eyes. But he probably couldn't see anything through the blur of good, hard sex. Lust was written all over his deliciously handsome face.

He increased the rhythm, pulling her into the orgasm they both craved. When it happened, she shook and shivered, tumbling into a hopeless abyss.

In the moments that followed, he released her arms, but he didn't lift his body from hers. He breathed heavily against her ear, his chest rising and falling against hers.

Libby feared that she might cry, like the grieving widow he kept accusing her of being. Now that the sex was over, she needed to untangle her limbs from his, to free herself from the beautiful weight of him. Trying to break the connection, she said, "You're getting heavy."

He raised his head and rolled off her. "Sorry about that." He sat up. "I have to take care of the condom, anyway. Messy things."

She nodded, needing the reprieve. "We should probably get dressed, before the sun comes up."

"We've still got time. But I suppose you're right." He grabbed his clothes off the stall door and left her alone.

Libby got up and put her clothes on. Matt was gone a bit longer than she expected, but he was probably checking on the mare and her foal.

He returned, and she asked, "Are Annie and the baby all right?"

"They're fine." He angled his head. "Are you all right? You seem sort of anxious."

If he only knew. "I just want to get the stall cleaned up before any of your ranch hands get here." She gestured to the blanket, the cider bottle, the plastic glasses.

"That'll only take a minute."

"It's better to be safe than sorry."

"Sure. Okay." He balled up the blanket. "Are you going to take a nap after we get back to the house?"

"No. I'm going to stay up." She didn't see how she would be able to sleep.

"I'm staying up, too. I can't wait until everyone sees the foal."

She nodded, as if that was her first priority, too. But for now, all she wanted was to protect her heart from the ache that was tearing her apart. Nothing was ever going to be right in Libby's world again, not if she couldn't find a way to stop loving Matt.

After breakfast, Matt and Libby took Chance to see the foal. Debra decided to stay behind. She was going to meet them there later, with Matt's mom and Lester. Matt didn't mind. He was enjoying it either way.

He hoisted Chance up so he could see the foal over the stall door. Chance was being his usual wiggleworm self, twisting and turning in Matt's arms.

Matt smiled and said, "You can help me name her."

The boy craned his neck. "Really? Truly? I can?"

"Absolutely. But since she's going to be registered with a quarter horse association, there are some guidelines we have to follow. We can only use a name that has a maximum of twenty characters. That includes letters, numbers and blank spaces. We can't use punctuation marks, either. Once we choose a name, I'll have to submit it to be sure there aren't any other horses with that exact name. If there are, then I'll have to change it up a bit."

Chance made a perplexed face. "That's a lot to think about."

"I know, but that's how it's done. Some people prefer to name their foal something that's composed of the sire's and dam's names. And some prefer to come up with something different, a name that sets the foal apart."

Chance looked even more perplexed. "I don't get it. What's a dam and a sire?"

"Oh, sorry." Matt had forgotten to define the lingo ahead of time. As easily as Chance had adapted to the ranch, he was still a city kid. "The sire is the father, and the dam is the mother."

Chance flashed a mischief-making grin. "Does that mean I can call my mom a dam, too?"

Matt couldn't help but laugh. Even Libby chuckled a little, before she shook her head and said, "Sorry, no. You can't call me that."

Matt was glad to see Libby smile. But she seemed distant. Ever since they'd made love earlier, she'd been behaving oddly. Even now, there was a glimmer of something unsettling in her eyes. Of course, he could be reading too much into it. They'd both been up all night, and sleep deprivation could do strange things to people. But he'd never been good at figuring women out, so he couldn't be sure.

"Who's the sire?" Chance asked, using the new term he'd learned. "Who's the foal's daddy?"

Matt replied, "His name is Promising Spirit. He's the stud that services my mares. Sometimes other people breed their mares to him, too."

"Why are you calling him a stud?" Chance scratched

his head, punctuating his confusion. "I thought he was a sire."

"It's sort of the same thing, except that he's a sire after the foals are born and a stud before. He's also called a stallion. Male horses that aren't used for breeding are called geldings. Also, boy horses are known as colts and girls as fillies, but that's only when they're young. Baby horses in general are referred to as foals. When they're between one and two years old, they're called yearlings."

"Wow. That's a lot to remember."

"It's easy once you get used to it. It's also something every cowboy should know."

"Then I'm gonna learn it, for sure." Chance puffed up his chest. Pinned to his shirt was a tin star, a toy sheriff's badge that had come from the ranch's gift store. "I'm gonna be the best cowboy ever."

Matt smiled and glanced over at Libby to get her reaction, but she wasn't looking at him or listening to Chance. She was watching the mare and the foal. When she turned and caught Matt eyeing her, she returned his gaze with an uncomfortable start. She was definitely acting strange. He couldn't question her about it, at least not in front of her son. But she was confusing the hell out of Matt.

"Can we start working on names now?" Chance asked.

Matt redirected his focus. "Absolutely. I was thinking that we could give her something associated with both the sire's and dam's names."

The boy made one of his puzzled faces. "How come the dam is called Annie Oakley? That sounds like a person's name."

Matt explained, "Annie Oakley was a real person, and the horse was named after her. Annie was a sharpshooter in the Old West. She performed with Buffalo Bill's Wild West. It was a show that traveled around, sort of like a circus. She was married to a guy named Frank E. Butler, and he was a marksman, too. There was also a famous Indian who appeared in the show. His name was Sitting Bull. He was a great warrior in his day, and he and Annie became friends. He nicknamed her Little Sure Shot."

Chance appeared to be taking it all in, listening intently to Matt's tale. After a minute of silence, he asked, "Are you from the same tribe as Sitting Bull?"

"No. He was Lakota Sioux, and I'm Cherokee. But I've always admired him."

"What did you say his nickname for Annie was?"

"Little Sure Shot."

"Can we name the foal something like that, except add something from the sire's name, too?"

Matt grinned. This kid was a natural. "What a great idea." He tossed out some combinations. "How about Little Spirit Shot? Or we could shorten it to Lil Spirit Shot? Or even Lil Shot of Spirit?"

"I like Lil Spirit Shot." Chance beamed, as bright and shiny as the badge he wore. "That's my favorite."

"Then that'll be our first choice. I'll check the registry and see if it's available, and we'll go from there."

"Okay." Chance turned toward Libby. "I just helped name the foal, Mom. Do you like what I picked?"

"It's wonderful. You're good with horses, in all sorts of ways." She smiled proudly at her son.

But Matt noticed that she still seemed out of sorts. He could see the faraway look that remained in her eyes, leaving him as confused as ever.

Eleven

Libby couldn't handle being around Matt, especially when he kept asking her if something was wrong. Her only solution was to say that she didn't feel well. So over the next few days, she faked being sick. Fatigue, chills, body aches: whatever she could drum up.

Her mom had been entertaining Chance, allowing Libby to rest. But she wasn't resting. Mostly she just stayed in her room, steeped in anxiety and hiding from Matt. The only time she emerged was when he was at work.

Today, Mom brought her breakfast, entering her room with a food tray. There was even a little daisy on it.

"The orange juice is fresh," her mother said. "Matt

thought the vitamin C might help. Oh, and the flower is from Chance. He picked it from the yard."

Feeling horribly guilty, Libby glanced at the meal. There were poached eggs and whole wheat toast, too. "That was sweet of them."

Mom placed the tray on the nightstand. "Are you feeling any better?"

"Not really." Libby was in bed, with the covers pulled up to her neck. She didn't know how she was ever going to feel normal again.

Her mom sat on the edge of the mattress. "You need to eat."

"I'm not very hungry." At least she wasn't faking that. She didn't have much of an appetite.

"Maybe just try the toast." Her mom handed her a slice.

Libby sat up and nibbled on it. She sipped the juice, too.

Her mom wasn't dressed. She still had on her pajamas. But unlike Libby, her hair was neatly combed, and she'd put on a smidgen of lipstick.

"Matt is taking care of Chance today," she said.

"Really? Matt's not working?" Libby assumed he would be leaving soon.

"He took the day off to spend it with Chance. They're going to a children's storytelling event on the ranch, where actors are portraying characters from the Old West. Chance is excited about it. There's going to be a woman dressed as Annie Oakley, and he wants to get her autograph."

"Oh, that's so cute." But it heightened Libby's guilt. Cheating the way she was, lying about having flu symptoms. She should be attending the event, too.

"Matt actually plans to take the rest of the week off. He wants to spend as much time with Chance as he can before we leave. I think he wants to keep an eye on you, too, and make sure you recover." Her mom's gaze bore into hers. "But you're not really sick, are you?"

Stunned by the accurate accusation, Libby tightened her hold on her glass. "Why would you say that?"

"Because you did this when you were little. Just once, when you were in kindergarten. Don't you remember?"

"No. What exactly did I do?"

"You pretended to be sick so you didn't have to go to school. There was a boy you liked, but he didn't like you back, and you were too upset to see him."

Suddenly Libby had a vague recollection of having a crush on a kid who made stupid faces at her. "Was his name Paul?"

"I don't know. It could have been. But the important part is that I convinced you to go to school the next day, to be brave and challenge your fears. And you did. You paraded into that classroom with your head held high, and you never backed away from anyone or anything again."

"This is different."

"No, it isn't. Whatever is wrong between you and Matt, you have to confront it. I can tell that you have feelings for him. I suspected it all along. I just didn't think it was my place to say anything until now."

So she hadn't fooled her mother, not one little bit. "Does Julie know, too?"

"She didn't notice it right away, but the more time she spent around you and Matt, the more she thought that something might be going on. That you two were romantically involved."

"I'm in love with him, Mom."

"Have you told him how you feel?"

"No." She put her juice aside. Her fingers were going numb from the iron grip she had on holding it. "But what's the point? He's not going to be able to cope with it, and he's not going to love me back."

"How do you know what he can or can't or will or won't do?"

"We made a deal not to fall in love."

Her mother furrowed her brow. "Was that his idea?"

"It was mine. But he readily agreed to it. He wants to get married again someday, but not to a widow. He thinks I'm too much like his ex-wife."

"Are you?"

"No. She wasn't ready to love again. She only married Matt for comfort. But I love him as much as I loved Becker."

"Then stand up for yourself and prove it."

"I don't know if I can."

"So you're not even going to try? That's not like you, Libby. You've always gone after what you wanted."

"Yes, and look at what I've lost in my life. How much more pain am I supposed to bear?"

"I'm so sorry." Her mom reached for her hand and held it. "But you're already hurting over Matt. Not telling him that you love him isn't taking the pain away, either. So just think about talking to him."

"I'll consider it. But I'm not making any promises." She wasn't a kindergartener being prodded to go back to school. And Matt wasn't a boy who'd been making stupid faces at her. He was the man she loved, on the heels of losing the husband she loved.

"I'm going to leave you alone now." Her mom stood and smoothed her pajamas. "But how about if I open the blinds? You shouldn't be sitting here in the dark."

Libby wanted to be immersed in darkness, to wallow in her pain, but she let her mother open the blinds anyway, allowing the sun to come spilling into the room.

Drenching her in light.

The following day, Libby decided to do it. To talk to Matt. To be brave. Her mom was right about confronting her feelings for him. Hiding out in bed wasn't helping.

Since he was at work, she texted him. She kept it short and simple, telling him that she was no longer ill and needed to see him. She suggested meeting at his cabin later. She chose that location because his house was too crowded, with her mom and Chance being there. She wanted as much privacy as possible.

He replied that he could be there at six and that he was looking forward to seeing her. He even included a happy face emoji in his text. He obviously thought this was going to be a nice get-together.

She took a long, hot shower and fixed herself up. Attired in a summer blouse and slim-fitting jeans, with her hair decorated with two shiny jeweled barrettes, she tried to look bright and breezy and confident. Like the happy face he'd sent.

But deep down, where it hurt, she was prepared for an emotional disaster. She didn't expect Matt to take her news lightly. If anything, he would probably panic and pull away from her. But at least he would know that she loved him. At this point, she just wanted him to know the truth.

She arrived at the cabin at a quarter to six. She didn't have a key, so she sat on the porch and waited.

Time passed slowly…one minute ticking into the next. When Matt's truck appeared, gravel crunching beneath its tires, her pulse jumped like a scared rabbit.

Could she do this? Could she say what she'd come here to say? Yes, she told herself. No matter how difficult it was, she could do it. She stood, determined to follow through.

Matt parked and climbed out of his truck. She admired the denim-clad, dusty-booted way in which he moved. The ultimate rancher, she thought. The long, tall country boy.

"Hey, Libby." He adjusted the brim of his hat. "You sure look pretty."

"Thank you." She reminded herself to breathe. He was nearing the porch steps.

When he reached the top, he said, "I'm so glad you're feeling better. I've been worried about you."

"I have a confession to make," she said, wanting to get it over with quickly. "I didn't have the flu. Or anything else anyone could catch." If her lovesick condition had been contagious, she would've infected him purposely, making him love her, making him want her for the rest of his life.

"So what was wrong with you?"

"I was just run-down." That was the easiest and fastest way for her to explain it until she gave him the full story. "But I'm stronger now." Or as strong as the moment would allow.

He jangled his keys and flashed what could only be described as a kissable smile. If only she could grab him and kiss him.

"Is this some sort of secret date?" he asked. "Are you going to take me inside and do wild things to me?"

"That's not why I'm here." But it was tempting, so darned tempting. "I need to tell you something."

His smile faded. "Is it about the book?"

"What? No." Kirby's biography was the last thing on her mind. And that troubled her, too. She'd lost sight of her goals, of convincing Matt to participate in the book. Yet that was the reason she'd come to the ranch, and now she'd gotten sidetracked by her feelings for him. "This isn't about your dad." She shifted her stance, her boots sounding on the wooden planks beneath her feet. "Can we go inside? I just want to say what I have to say before I lose my nerve, and I don't want to talk out here."

He unlocked the door. "You're starting to freak me out, Libby."

And it was only going to get worse, she thought.

They went into the cabin, and she made a beeline for the sofa, needing to sit. He took a chair across from her, as if he was leery of sitting next to her. He was already pulling away, and she hadn't even told him what was going on yet.

She took a big, noisy breath, and he watched her with a taut expression.

She said, "I broke our deal, Matt. I know we agreed not to fall in love, but I'm in love with you. Irrecoverably, frighteningly in love with you."

He just stared at her, as if she was speaking a foreign language he didn't understand.

Libby glanced up at the ceiling, praying for divine intervention. But she didn't get any.

Matt finally spoke, his voice rattled and gruff. "I can't believe you…"

She couldn't fault him for his disbelief, for not being able to form the rest of his words. She said, "I didn't mean to blindside you. I blindsided myself, too. I stayed in bed, pretending to be sick, not knowing how to face this. But I couldn't hide from you anymore. I had to tell you."

"What do you want from me?" He tensed as if he'd

been sucker punched. "What is it that I'm supposed to do?"

"I'm not asking you to do anything."

He gave her a bewildered look. "You love me, but you don't want to be with me?"

"No, I do. I mean, I…" Now she was struggling to find her words. She took a second to compose her next sentence. "I would spend the rest of my life with you if I could." She wasn't going to lie about that. She had to express how she felt, to let honesty be her guide.

"So in your estimation, how would that work?" His voice was still rattled, still wrecked with emotion. "Chance is still so hung up on his father. If I married you, I couldn't replace Becker for you or your son." He stood and moved away from his chair. "Would you expect me to exist in Becker's shadow, like I did with Greg?"

"It wouldn't be like that." She remained seated, watching him pace. "It wouldn't be a competition between you and Becker. You'd be my husband, the man I'd be devoting my heart to. And you'd be Chance's father in every way."

"But Becker's memory would still be there. I don't think I can do it, Libby. I can't go down that road again. If I let myself love you, it would tear me apart."

"If you *let* yourself love me?" She leaned forward, her heart teetering on the edge of pain, of hope, of determination. "That sounds like you're capable of falling in love with me, too."

He stopped pacing, stalled in the middle of the

room, staring at her, as if the walls were threatening to close in on him. "What difference does it make? It would never work between us."

"Maybe it could, if you let it." She ached for him, for herself, for Chance, for the life they could have together. "I understand what you went through with Sandy and the twins, but it wouldn't be the same." She softly added, "I love you the way a wife should love a husband. And Becker would be happy for me if I married you. He would want me to have a full and joyous life, and he would want you to become Chance's father. Becker wouldn't overshadow you—"

"I'm sorry," he interrupted. "If we tried it and it didn't work out, it would be devastating for all of us." He didn't move from the spot where he stood. He seemed riveted to the floor, waiting for the walls to crush him, to break him in two. "I can't put myself in a position like that. Or you or Chance."

And she couldn't sit here and beg him to love her, if Matt loving her was even possible. "You're right. If you can't love me back, it won't work between us. I need to go on with my life, and you go on with yours."

"That's what we agreed on when we started our affair."

"I know." That was the bargain they'd struck, the deal she'd broken. Her eyes turned watery. "But when the foal was born, I imagined having my next child with you. And it scared me. It scared me so much. But I still wanted it."

"Don't cry." He took a cautious step toward her. "Please, don't cry."

She stood, warding him off, trying to keep him away from her. "I need to get some air."

She turned and headed for the door, rushing onto the porch and bursting into the tears he'd asked her not to cry.

Matt's head was reeling. How was he supposed to think clearly, knowing that Libby loved him; that she wanted to marry him; that she longed to have his babies and give Chance little brothers or sisters?

And now she was outside, probably bawling her eyes out. Deep, sobbing tears, he thought, like the kind Sandy used to cry.

Matt couldn't leave her out there alone. He couldn't bear to see her hurting more than she already was. He was hurting, too, picturing the life she'd described. But it was a false dream, a fairy tale that couldn't possibly come true.

He grabbed a box of tissues from the bathroom and went onto the patio. She sat on the porch steps, with her head in her hands. He sat next to her, and she lifted her head. Her face was covered in tears.

He handed her the tissues. "I thought you might need these."

"Thank you." She dabbed at her eyes. "I haven't cried like this since Becker died." She sniffed through her tears. "I feel like someone is dying all over again."

So did Matt. The death of the kind of man he wished

he could be. "You deserve someone who can make you happy, who can give you what you need, who doesn't have my hang-ups."

She sniffed again, her voice soft, sad. "You're encouraging me to find someone else someday?"

"Yes." But when he envisioned her with another man, he got a knot in the center of his chest, clawing its way to his heart. It was torture because the fear of keeping her, of making her his bride, incited the same tangled feeling. "I'm going to go away for the rest of the week." He couldn't stay at the ranch. He needed to escape.

"Where will you go?"

Anywhere, nowhere. "I'll do a road trip." He would simply drive to wherever his aimlessness took him. "You can keep staying at my house while I'm gone."

She clutched the tissue box to her chest. "That isn't necessary."

"It is to me. I want you to stay there." He waited an agonizing beat before he said, "When I go back to the house to grab some things, I'll tell Chance and your mom that I have to go away on business."

"There's no point in creating a story for my mother. I already told her that I love you."

He winced. "Does my mother know?"

"Not the whole story. Not yet. But she suspected that something was going on between us, so I'm sure my mom will tell her."

"They're going to think I'm an idiot." And he was, no doubt, for letting Libby and her son go. But he'd already tried creating that type of family with Sandy and the twins, and he'd failed miserably at it. So how would it be any different this time?

"No one is going to think badly of you." She blew out a sigh. "And you don't have to leave town, either. I can pack up and go to Kirby's early."

"No." He couldn't stand the thought of her spending extra time at his father's. He already hated that she was going there. "Just stay at my house, please. Let Chance enjoy the ranch for a few more days."

"He's going to miss you."

"I'll miss him, too." Suddenly he felt as if he was abandoning Libby and Chance in the way Kirby had abandoned him. But he couldn't blame his dad. Matt was destroying his relationship with Libby on his own. "I really suck at this."

Her breaths came out choppy. "I obviously do, too."

"No, you don't." He wanted to reach for her, to hold her, to soothe her. But he didn't have the right to take her in his arms. Still, he moved a bit closer, trying to inhale the scent of her skin.

She reacted by scooting farther away from him. But he understood that she was only trying to protect herself from the guy who was breaking her heart.

She said, "We need to go back to the house and get the rest of this over with."

"Yes, we do." There was nothing else left to do, except separate from each other for good.

It was over.

Matt had left hours ago, and now Libby was suffering through self-imposed bouts of romantic torture, the pain of wandering through his house, of touching everything he'd touched.

She gazed out the living room window, wishing he would come back. But his truck didn't reappear out of the blue. The driveway was as empty as her soul.

"Are you sure you're not sick no more?" Chance asked.

She turned and looked at her son. He was playing a video game that Matt had given him, where the players participated in rodeo events. At the moment, it was bull riding.

"I'm doing okay," she said.

"You don't seem better." He leaned into the game, his gaze fixed on the giant TV screen. "Are you sad 'cause Matt had to go away?"

Her heart clenched. Her six-year-old was far more observant than she'd expected him to be. Everyone was, it seemed, when it came to her and Matt. "Yes."

"Me, too. I wish he was still here." The virtual cowboy Chance was maneuvering fell off the bull and scrambled to his feet. He put the machine on pause. "Wanna play? I can teach you the way Matt taught me. It might make you feel better."

"Thanks, honey. But I'll just watch you." She sat beside him. "You know I'm not a gamer."

He didn't restart it. "Matt's one of my all-time favorite people."

"Mine, too." She wanted to stay in Texas forever, on this ranch, in this house, with Matt by her side.

"He said I can call him if I ever need anything."

"He did?" Her heart clenched again. "That was nice of him." Matt hadn't made the same offer to her. But his relationship with her was far more complex than the one he'd built with Chance.

"I'd have to use your phone if I ever called him. Or Nana's or somebody else's. Unless you want to buy me one."

She shook her head, being the responsible parent she was supposed to be. "Nice try. But you're not getting a smartphone, at least not for a while."

He made a face. Then he asked, "Are we still going to Kirby Talbot's house after we leave here?"

"Yes, we're still going. He's going to sing you the song you're named after, remember?"

"Oh, yeah." Chance grinned. "That'll be fun. Do you like having him as your book boss?"

"I absolutely do. He's nice to work for. But I also have an editor who's involved in it. So I guess you could say that I have two book bosses." Of course, she couldn't tell Chance that Kirby was Matt's father or how pivotal their past was to the project. Her son was too young to be dragged into something like that.

Libby reflected on her job and the decision she'd made. Considering everything else that had happened, she'd given up on trying to interview Matt. She couldn't force him to be part of his father's biography any more than she could force him to love her.

"Are there going to be any kids at Kirby's for me to play with?" Chance asked.

"Not that I know of." Kirby didn't have any grand-children. None of his sons, including Matt, had fa-thered any children. "But you and Nana are going to go sightseeing in Nashville while Kirby and I work on the book. Nana is going to take you to Memphis, too, on a big fancy bus." Her mother had already booked the tour. "She wants to see Graceland. That's where Elvis Presley used to live."

"I wish Matt was going to do all of that stuff with us."

So did Libby. But again, that wasn't something she could discuss with her son. She quickly asked, "Are you hungry? I can fix you some lunch."

"Okay." He restarted the game.

Libby went into the kitchen and opened the fridge. She removed the sandwich fixings, trying to keep her restless mind off Matt. But it wasn't working. He was all she could think about.

She fumbled with the food, struggling to make a simple sandwich. This wasn't the time to dwell on un-requited love. But she couldn't seem to shake it from her shattered heart.

Libby was lost without Matt.

Twelve

When Matt returned to his house, Libby and her family were long gone. There was nothing from Libby. No notes. No mementos. But he hadn't expected as much. Chance, however, had left him a brightly colored crayon drawing on the fridge. It depicted a stick figure of Chance roping red-eyed Stanley with a much taller stick figure of Matt standing nearby. The kid had captured them with happy expressions on their faces.

Matt was anything but happy. Being on the road, driving into an endless horizon, sleeping in off-the-beaten-path motels had been lonely as hell. But this was worse. His house felt like a big, empty echo. But that was the reason he'd stopped living here before.

After Sandy and the girls had left, he couldn't stand being here alone.

And now he was alone again. But it wasn't Sandy and the twins he was missing. It was Libby and Chance.

He went into his bedroom and tossed his overnight bag on the bed. Going back to the cabin wouldn't do him any good. That location would only remind him of Libby, too.

She was everywhere: in the air, in the flowers, in the trees, in the hills that surrounded the ranch, in the sparkle of sunlight that seeped through his windows. But mostly, she was inside him.

Sweet, beautiful Libby.

He'd rejected her out of fear. Afraid that if he married her, their union would fail. That he would be reliving the turmoil with Sandy. But Libby had kept telling him that she wasn't Sandy.

And she was right. They were two completely different women, with separate feelings, with opposite needs. Libby loved him, truly loved him, in a way that Sandy never could have.

Libby longed to be the girl of his dreams, to become his forever wife, to share her son with him, to have more children together. Yet Matt had been so fixated on his fears, he'd walked away from the best thing that had ever happened to him.

Suddenly, it was so damned clear. And so were his feelings. He loved Libby, too. He absolutely loved her.

Libby had already explained how she felt. She even

told him that Becker would be happy for her if she and Matt became a couple. That he would want them to be together.

Clearly, Becker had been a kind and caring man, deserving of the family he had. And now Matt wanted to follow in his footsteps. If he married Libby, he wouldn't be competing with Becker. He would be taking over where Becker left off. It was a blessing that was being given to him.

Matt hadn't been able to soothe Sandy's soul because they didn't belong together. But Matt and Libby clicked. She was right for him. Someday, maybe, Sandy would find someone who was right for her, too, who could help her make peace with losing Greg. Or maybe she would have to travel that road alone, as Libby had done before she'd met Matt. But one thing Matt knew for certain was that he loved Libby as much as she loved him.

He closed his eyes, feeling free and strong. But when he reopened them and caught his reflection in a mirror from across the room, he still saw a troubled version of himself.

Because there was another obstacle, he thought, one that had been there all along. Matt's father.

How was he going to start over with Libby if he didn't start over with Kirby, if he didn't give his old man a chance?

Matt cursed to himself. Could he do it? Could he let bygones be bygones? Could he give his father an open invitation into his life?

Libby believed that he needed to make peace with his dad. She saw Kirby as a man who deserved to be forgiven, who wanted to make up for the past.

But Matt still hated him. He still wanted to rage at his dad for the pain he caused. But was that the example he wanted to set for Chance? Or the future children he and Libby could have? Did he want to deliver a message of anger and hate?

No, he thought. He didn't. If he was going to create a strong, solid family of his own, then he had to let Kirby be part of it, too. No matter how difficult it was, Matt didn't have a choice, not if he intended to be with Libby.

No doubt about it, Matt was going to have to book a trip to Nashville to see Libby, to tell her how he felt, to open himself up to her. He was going to have to see his father, too, and dig down deep to forgive him.

But first he needed to take some time to shop for an engagement ring. When he proposed to Libby, he wanted to do it with the biggest, fanciest, shiniest diamond he could find.

Something as dazzling as the woman he loved.

Libby stared at the mind-blowing text she'd just received from Matt. He was in Nashville, and he wanted to know if she would come to his hotel room. So they could talk privately. So he could say something extremely important to her. But it had to be in person. He couldn't do it over the phone.

She agreed to see him. But while she was getting

ready, she worried herself sick. Why had he traveled all this way? And why was it so imperative that it be in person? Was it about the book? Or was it much more personal?

Was it possible that he loved her, too, that those were the words he was going to say? She hoped and prayed they were. But was she being unrealistic? Longing for something that wasn't going to happen? The last time she saw Matt, he insisted that it would never work between them.

She couldn't talk to anyone else about it. She wouldn't dare say something to Kirby. He didn't even know that she and Matt had been lovers, and this certainly wasn't the time to tell him. Libby couldn't talk to her mom, either. She and Chance were on their overnight trip to Memphis, getting their Elvis on. No way was she going to disturb them with a high-anxiety phone call.

Alone in her thoughts, she glanced around the luxurious guesthouse where she was staying. Kirby's enormous compound offered a parklike setting with a stream that ran through the middle. He lived in the main house, a mansion he'd renovated to fit his needs. He'd also built extra houses for family and friends, along with a recording studio. Kirby had everything he wanted, except a relationship with Matt.

Once again, Libby fretted about seeing Matt and what he was going to say. If she pinned her hopes on him loving her and she was wrong, she would fall apart all over again.

She finished getting dressed in a lacy sundress and

gold sandals and climbed into her rental car. Matt's hotel was actually quite close. She assumed he'd chosen it because of its location, making it more convenient for them to meet. It was a newly renovated resort, and he was staying in room 614.

Once Libby arrived, she took the elevator to the sixth floor. It felt like the longest ride of her life, with other people stopping on other floors. Her stomach was overrun with butterflies.

When she exited the elevator, she followed the room number signs. Matt's room was near the end of the hallway. She took a deep breath and knocked on his door.

He answered with an anxious smile, looking as nervous as she felt. But he looked stylish, too. He wore a swanky Western shirt, crisply laundered jeans and freshly polished boots.

"Come in." He stepped back.

She crossed the threshold, and he closed the door. They stood a bit awkwardly, with neither of them moving forward to initiate a hug. But they hadn't hugged goodbye the last time they'd seen each other, either. They hadn't touched since the night they'd made love in the barn, and that seemed like an eternity ago.

"This is a nice place," she said, trying to break the ice. His suite was artfully designed, with a sitting room, kitchen, dining cove, bathroom and bedroom. The balcony overlooked a big, flourishing garden.

"Do you want to go out there?" He gestured to the balcony.

Libby nodded, and they proceeded outside. She was grateful for the fresh air. She was having trouble catching her breath.

They sat at a mosaic-topped table, and she said, "The garden is beautiful."

"You're the one who's beautiful." He traced the pattern on the table with restless hands. "I'm so sorry that I hurt you. That I turned you away. I missed you so badly when we were apart. I came home to an empty house and knew what a mistake I'd made."

She perched on the edge of her chair. Was he heading toward the admission of love she'd been hoping and praying to hear? And if he was, could she be certain that he meant it? That he wasn't going to hurt her again? Or reject her if things got too difficult?

He continued, his voice deep and clear, "I don't want to live the rest of my life without you. I love you, Libby."

There it was. He'd said it. But she hesitated to respond.

He nervously asked, "Did I do something wrong? Have your feelings for me changed? Please, Libby, tell me what you're thinking."

"I'm just a little scared. Worried about all of the stuff you said before."

"I was scared, too, when I said those things. But once I came home to an empty house, I searched my soul and worked through my fears. I love you. I honestly do. And I don't want anything to ever keep us apart again."

She blinked back tears and reached across the table for his hand. "I love you, too. You're all I've been thinking about."

His fingertips connected with hers. "I should have listened to you from the start. You were right about everything, about how different you are from Sandy, about how I needed to stop comparing you to her."

She searched his gaze, losing herself in those whiskey eyes. Just holding his hand was electrifying. "So you're never going to compare me to her again?"

"No. And I'm not going to punish you for staying close to Becker's memory. I want Chance to grow up with happy thoughts about his father. But I want to become Chance's daddy, too."

Matt stood and came around to her chair. He got down on bended knee, and the tears she'd been banking began to fall.

He removed a small jewelry box from his pocket. Inside was a halo ring, a gold band encrusted with multicolored stones and set with a big, bright, round-cut diamond, surrounded by even more diamonds.

He softly asked, "Will you marry me?"

She nodded, her voice cracking when she replied, "Yes. A thousand times, yes."

He put the ring on her finger, and it fit perfectly. Everything was perfect, she thought, so much more than she could have imagined.

"It's absolutely gorgeous," she said. "How did you know my size?"

"I didn't. I guessed what it was."

"You guessed right."

He came to his feet. "Because I've been memorizing you, so I have a detailed picture in my mind."

She stood and kissed him. His mouth was warm against hers. So was his body. Those big strong arms held her tenderly close. She'd been memorizing him, too.

Once the kiss ended, he said, "I'm going to take this as far as I can go. I'm going to participate in the book, and I'm going to do my damnedest to make to peace with Kirby, to find the power to forgive him."

She started. "Oh, my God. You are?"

"I can't keep letting the pain from my childhood fester. Not if I want to be the kind of man our kids can be proud of."

He couldn't have said anything more right, more perfect. "Our kids? As in plural?"

"You said that you wanted to have a baby with me." He nuzzled her cheek. "But I want to wait until after we're married. I want to do this the traditional way."

She nuzzled him right back. "That works for me. We can plan everything just right. We can have the ceremony on your ranch."

"With everyone we love there. You can invite Becker's family, if you want to. That would be nice for Chance, wouldn't it?"

This proposal kept getting better and better. "It would be amazing for him to have all of us together in one place. Thank you so much for thinking of him."

"He's going to be my son. I want what's best for him."

"You're just what he needs, Matt." She couldn't have asked for a better father for her child. "You're what I need, too."

"We're going to be a family, Libby, for the rest of our lives. And if you need to spend more time at Kirby's to finish the book, that's okay, too. I'm not going to stand in your way." He swept her up and carried her inside.

She wrapped her arms around his neck. Matt's support meant everything to her.

He hauled her straight to the bedroom, deposited her on the bed and removed her sandals. "Stay here. I'm going to fix us a special drink."

She felt giddy. She even wiggled her toes. "I'm not going anywhere."

He left, and she waited for him, with the diamonds he'd given her glittering on her finger. To Libby, the ring was a symbol of her future, of her shiny new life with Matt. She was glad that he'd chosen something so bright and colorful.

He returned in his bare feet, with two cocktail glasses rimmed with marshmallow fluff and crushed-up pieces of graham crackers. The drinks themselves were a creamy mocha color. He got into bed and handed her one.

She smiled. "A s'mores martini, I presume?"

"Yes, ma'am. Today is August tenth. National S'mores Day. I figured it would be a great day to get engaged."

He'd obviously skipped the celebration on the ranch to come here and be with her. "Maybe we can choose this as our wedding date, too, for next summer. We can combine it with the party you always have at the ranch."

"A chocolate-themed wedding?" He clinked his glass with hers. "It doesn't get any sweeter than that."

She sipped her martini and moaned. The flavor was rich and smooth and sexy. "What's in this?"

"Marshmallow vodka and chocolate liqueur. It's as fun to make as it is to drink."

"Do you have to shake it in one of those glamorous cocktail shakers?"

"Yep." He waggled his eyebrows. "It's very James Bond."

After they consumed every delicious drop, they rolled over the bed, kissing and touching and peeling off each other's clothes. They both had marshmallow fluff all over their lips. She wasn't sure what Bond would think of that.

But Libby loved it. She was naked with the cowboy of her dreams, and they had the sweetest, most romantic, most erotic sex possible. For now nothing mattered but being together. Just the two of them, making up for lost time with a lifetime of commitment between them.

Thirteen

Matt entered his father's mansion with Libby by his side. It was surreal, being in the house where Kirby lived, where Matt's brothers had grown up. The entire compound was as spectacular as he always imagined it would be. As a kid, he used to fantasize about coming here.

There was a sweeping staircase, hardwood floors and windows at every turn. It was an old plantation-style house with gold records lining the walls. Matt wasn't surprised that Kirby had them prominently displayed or that they were one of the first things you saw when you went inside.

His dad was expecting him. Matt had called Kirby from the hotel, giving him a condensed version of what was going on. That Libby and Matt were a couple. That Matt was going to participate in the book. That he was accepting Kirby's offer to get to know each other again.

Kirby's maid, who introduced herself as June, escorted Matt and Libby to the parlor. They waited for Kirby there. Libby sat on a velvet settee, but Matt was too anxious to sit. He stood tall and straight, his gaze fixed on the double doors. They were open, with an extravagant view of the foyer.

Someone soon appeared, but it wasn't Kirby. It was June again, bringing in a pitcher of sweet tea and three tall glasses.

After June left, Matt turned to look at Libby. She sent him a reassuring smile. But Matt was still anxious.

He said, "You'd think my dad would have already been here, waiting for us, instead of us waiting for him."

"He's probably as nervous as you are."

"Either that or he just wants to make a grand entrance."

Libby poured herself a glass of tea. "He is a showman. But this is a big day for the two of you. Are you sure you don't want to meet with him alone? I can go to the guesthouse where I've been staying and you can text me when the meeting is over."

"No way. I want you here." She was his inspiration, his lover, his friend, his fiancée—the person who'd helped him reach this point in his life. "I couldn't do this without you."

She nodded, and they both went silent.

Kirby finally came through the doorway, with his signature black clothes and country-star swagger. But he didn't speak. He just stared at Matt.

Matt stared back. He'd seen recent photos and videos of his dad on TV, in magazines and on the internet. He knew Kirby had aged and that his hair and beard were now threaded with gray. But seeing him in person created a gut-wrenching feeling. Matt wanted to turn and walk away. But he squared his shoulders and said, "Hey, Dad," instead.

Kirby moved closer to him. "Damn. Look at you. It's been so long since I've seen you. I might not even recognize you if it wasn't for your eyes."

Nearly two decades had passed since their last encounter. Matt was bound to change after all of that time. "I grew up."

"I'll say." There was an expression of awe on Kirby's face. "You're as tall as me."

"And just as ornery," Matt said. He couldn't help but throw that out there.

His old man smiled and reached out to hug him. Matt tensed for a moment, but he thought about the future, about his life with Libby, and he relaxed. He'd promised himself he was going to make this work with his dad. No more hatred. No more anger.

"I'm so sorry for what I did to you," Kirby said. "You deserved so much better. Please forgive me."

"I do forgive you." Matt was ready to move forward, to be Kirby Talbot's son. The hug ended, and Matt stepped back, needing to catch his breath. "But I'm going to be honest in the book. If I tell my side of the story, then I need to tell it truthfully."

"That's what I want you to do. I wouldn't expect any less from you."

Matt could feel Libby watching them. He glanced her way, and she smiled at him. She'd been smiling at him all day, making him feel strong and secure.

Nonetheless, Matt said to Kirby, "I'm not thrilled about how the press is going to hound me once they find out I'm your son."

His dad nodded. "I understand. It's not easy being in the public eye. Maybe we can do some interviews together. That will take some of the pressure off you. We might even want to consider making the announcement before the book is released. I can talk to the publisher about it, and they can work with my publicist on scheduling the interviews."

"Sure. We can do it that way. Promoting the book ahead of time will probably get people more interested in reading it." For Libby's sake, Matt wanted his father's biography to be a success.

Kirby shifted his feet. His boots were adorned with sterling silver tips. He'd always worn fancy garb, on and off stage. Matt was just glad that he wasn't hiding behind a pair of sunglasses, the way he used to do when Matt was a kid.

"We're going to have to arrange a meeting between you and your brothers," Kirby said. "Neither of them is in town right now. Tommy is on tour, and Brandon is away on business. But they both want to meet you."

"I know. Libby told me. She's been championing all of this since the beginning."

Kirby shot Libby a superstar grin. "And now you're together." He turned his attention back to Matt. "I'm happy you found each other, and that I could be part of it. Without the book, you two wouldn't have met."

Really? Matt thought. His old man was taking credit for being their matchmaker? "That's quite an ego you got there, Dad."

Kirby chuckled. "That's what everyone who knows me says about me. That I'm the most egotistical guy around. But I'll work on being more humble."

"That's going to be difficult for you." Matt's father wouldn't know humble if bit him in the balls. But Matt was going to accept his arrogant old man, faults and all. "I appreciate the effort, though."

Kirby went serious. "I want you to be proud of me, son."

Matt responded with affection. "I'm proud of this moment, of what we've accomplished so far. I can tell how much this reunion matters to you. It's important to me, too."

"Thank you. Having you become part of my family means everything to me. We have so much catching up to do, so many gaps to fill. I hope you'll be inviting me to your wedding."

"I definitely will." He wasn't going to leave his dad or his brothers or anyone else out of it. "But you'll have to come to Texas, to my ranch, because that where it's going to be."

"I'll be there with bells on." Kirby waved Libby over, bringing her into the fold. "Come show me the ring this boy put on your finger. It's already blinding me from here."

She hopped off the settee and dashed over to them. When she held out her hand, Kirby whistled. "That's some rock." He smiled at Matt. "You did a wonderful job, with the ring, with the woman. You're going to be a hell of a husband, and a damned fine father to her son, too." Kirby rocked on his heels. "And how amazing is it that he was named after one of my songs?"

Matt nearly laughed. There went his dad's ego again. But it did seem to make a poetic kind of sense. "Especially since Chance is going to become your grandson."

"I know, right? And what a great kid he is."

"He's the best." Matt couldn't wait to tell Chance that he and Libby were getting married. Chance would also have to be told that Kirby was Matt's father. But for now, Matt wanted to take it one day at a time.

Libby leaned into him, and he put his arm around her, holding her close. Kirby smiled at them in a paternal way, and Matt thanked the Creator for bringing peace to his life. And love, he thought, so much love and support from Libby. Matt continued to hold her, grateful for the journey that had just begun.

* * * * *

*Can a former bad boy and the woman
he never forgot find true love during one
unforgettable Christmas?
Find out in CHRISTMASTIME COWBOY,
the sizzling new COPPER RIDGE novel from
New York Times bestselling author Maisey Yates.
Read on for your sneak peek...*

LIAM DONNELLY WAS nobody's favorite.

Though being a favorite in their household growing up would never have meant much, Liam was confident that as much as both of his parents disdained
their younger son, Alex, they hated Liam more.

And as much as his brothers loved him—or whatever you wanted to call their brand of affection—Liam
knew he wasn't the one they'd carry out if there was a
house fire. That was fine, too.

It wasn't self-pity. It was just a fact.

But while he wasn't anyone's particular favorite,
he knew he was at least one person's least favorite.

Sabrina Leighton hated him with every ounce of
her beautiful, petite being. Not that he blamed her.
But, considering they were having a business meeting today, he did hope that she could keep some of the
hatred bottled up.

Liam got out of his truck and put his cowboy hat

on, surveying his surroundings. The winery spread was beautiful, with a large, picturesque house overlooking the grounds. The winery and the road leading up to it were carved into an Oregon mountainside. Trees and forest surrounded the facility on three sides, creating a secluded feeling. Like the winery was part of another world. In front of the first renovated barn was a sprawling lawn and a path that led down to the river. There was a seating area there and Liam knew that during the warmer months it was a nice place to hang out. Right now, it was too damned cold, and the damp air that blew up from the rushing water sent a chill straight through him.

He shoved his hands in his pockets and kept on walking. There were three rustic barns on the property that they used for weddings and dinners, and one that had been fully remodeled into a dining and tasting room.

He had seen the new additions online. He hadn't actually been to Grassroots Winery in the past thirteen years. That was part of the deal. The deal that had been struck back when Jamison Leighton was still owner of the place.

Back when Liam had been nothing more than a good-for-nothing, low-class troublemaker with a couple of misdemeanors to his credit.

Times changed.

Liam might still be all those things at heart, but he was also a successful businessman. And Jamison Leighton no longer owned Grassroots.

Some things, however, hadn't changed. The presence of Sabrina Leighton being one of them.

It had been thirteen years. But he couldn't pretend he thought everything was all right and forgiven. Not considering the way she had reacted when she had seen him at Ace's bar the past few months.

Small towns. Like everybody was at the same party and could only avoid each other for so long.

If it wasn't at the bar, they would most certainly end up at a four-way stop at the same time, or in the same aisle at the grocery store.

But today's meeting would not be accidental. Today's meeting was planned. He wondered if something would get thrown at him. It certainly wouldn't be the first time.

He walked across the gravel lot and into the dining room. It was empty, since the facility—a rustic barn with a wooden chandelier hanging in the center—had yet to open for the day. There was a bar with stools positioned at the front, and tables set up around the room. Back when he had worked here, there had been one basic tasting room, and nowhere for anyone to sit. Most of the wine had been sent out to retail stores for sale, rather than making the winery itself some kind of destination.

He wondered when all of that had changed. He imagined it had something to do with Lindy, the new owner and ex-wife of Jamison Leighton's son, Damien. As far as Liam knew, and he knew enough—considering he didn't get involved with business ventures without figuring out what he was getting into—Damien had drafted the world's dumbest prenuptial agreement. At least, it was dumb for a man who clearly had problems keeping his dick in his pants.

Though why Sabrina was still working at the winery when her sister-in-law had current ownership, and her brother had been deposed, and her parents were—from what he had read in public records—apoplectic about the loss of their family legacy, he didn't know. But he assumed he would find out. At about the same time he found out whether or not something was going to get thrown at his head.

The door from the back opened, and he gritted his teeth. Because, no matter how prepared he felt philosophically to see Sabrina, he knew that there would be impact. There always was. A damned funny thing, that one woman could live in the back of his mind the way she had for so long. That no matter how many years or how many women he put between them, she still burned bright and hot in his memory.

That no matter that he had steeled himself to run into her—because he knew how small towns worked—the impact was like a brick to the side of his head every single time.

She appeared a moment after the door opened, looking severe. Overly so. Her blond hair was pulled back into a high ponytail, and she was wearing a black sheath dress that went down past her knees but conformed to curves that were more generous than they'd been thirteen years ago.

In a good way.

"Hello, Liam," she said, her tone impersonal. Had she not used his first name, it might have been easy to pretend that she didn't know who he was.

"Sabrina."

"Lindy told me that you wanted to talk about a potential joint venture. And since that falls under my jurisdiction as manager of the tasting room, she thought we might want to work together."

Now she was smiling.

The smile was so brittle it looked like it might crack her face.

"Yes, I'm familiar with the details. Particularly since this venture was my idea." He let a small silence hang there for a beat before continuing. "I'm looking at an empty building on the end of Main Street. It would be more than just a tasting room. It would be a small café with some retail space."

"How would it differ from Lane Donnelly's store? She already offers specialty foods."

"Well, we would focus on Grassroots wine and Laughing Irish cheese. Also, I would happily purchase products from Lane's to give the menu a local focus. The café would be nothing big. Just a small lunch place with wine. Very limited selection. Very specialty. But I feel like in a tourist location, that's what you want."

"Great," she said, her smile remaining completely immobile.

He took that moment to examine her more closely. The changes in her face over the years. She was more beautiful now than she had been at seventeen. Her slightly round, soft face had refined in the ensuing years, her cheekbones now more prominent, the angle of her chin sharper.

Her eyebrows looked different, too. When she'd been a teenager, they'd been thinner, rounder. Now they were a bit stronger, more angular.

"Great," he returned. "I guess we can go down and have a look at the space sometime this week. Gage West is the owner of the property, and he hasn't listed it yet. Handily, my sister-in-law is good friends with his wife. Both of my sisters-in-law, actually. So I got the inside track on that."

Her expression turned bland. "How impressive."

She sounded absolutely unimpressed. "It wasn't intended to be impressive. Just useful."

She sighed slowly. "Did you have a day of the week in mind to go view the property? Because I really am very busy."

"Are you?"

"Yes," she responded, that smile spreading over her face again. "This is a very demanding job, plus I do have a life."

She stopped short of saying exactly what that life entailed.

"Too busy to do this, which is part of your actual job?" he asked.

On the surface she looked calm, but he could sense a dark energy beneath that spoke of a need to savage him. "I had my schedule sorted out for the next couple of weeks. This is coming together more quickly than expected."

"I'll work something out with Gage and give Lindy a call, how about that?"

"You don't have to call Lindy. I'll give you my phone number. You can call or text me directly."

She reached over to the counter and took a card from the rustic surface, extending her hand toward him. He reached out and took the card, their fingertips brushing as they made the handoff.

And he felt it. Straight down to his groin, where he had always felt things for her, even though it was impossible. Even though he was all wrong for her. And even though now they were doing a business deal together, and she looked like she would cheerfully chew through his flesh if given half the chance.

She might be smiling, but he didn't trust that smile. He was still waiting. Waiting for her to shout recriminations at him now that they were alone. Every other time he had encountered her over the past four months it had been in public. Twice in Ace's bar, and once walking down the street, where she had made a very quick sharp left to avoid walking past him.

It had not been subtle, and it had certainly not spoken of somebody who was over the past.

So his assumption had been that if the two of them were ever alone she was going to let him have it. But she didn't. Instead, she gave him that card and then began to look…bored.

"Did you need anything else?" she asked.

"Not really. Though I have some spreadsheet information that you might want to look over. Ideas that I have for the layout, the menu. It is getting a little ahead of ourselves, in case we end up not liking the venue."

"You've been to look at the venue already, haven't you?" It was vaguely accusatory.

"I have been there, yes. But again, I believe in preparedness. I was hardly going to get very deep into this if I didn't think it was viable. Personally, I'm interested in making sure that we have diverse interests. The economy doesn't typically favor farms, Sabrina. And that is essentially what my brothers and I have. I expect an uphill fight to make that place successful."

She tilted her head to the side. "Like you said, you do your research."

Her friendliness was beginning to slip. And he waited. For something else. For something to get thrown at him. It didn't happen.

"That I do. Take these," he said, handing her the folder that he was holding on to. He made sure their fingers didn't touch this time. "And we'll talk next week."

Then he turned and walked away from her, and he resisted the strong impulse to turn back and get one more glance at her. It wasn't the first time he had resisted that.

He had a feeling it wouldn't be the last.

As soon as Liam walked out of the tasting room, Sabrina let out a breath that had been killing her to keep in. A breath that contained about a thousand insults and recriminations. And more than a few very colorful swear word combinations. A breath that nearly burned her throat, because it was full of so many sharp and terrible things.

She lifted her hands to her face and realized they were shaking. It had been thirteen years. Why did he still affect her like this? Maybe, just maybe, if she had ever found a man who made her feel even half of what Liam did, she wouldn't have such a hard time dealing with him. The feelings wouldn't be so strong.

But she hadn't. So that supposition was basically moot.

The worst part was the tattoos. He'd had about three when he'd been nineteen. Now they covered both of his arms, and she had the strongest urge to make them as familiar to her as the original tattoos had been. To memorize each and every detail about them.

The tree was the one that really caught her attention. The Celtic knots, she knew, were likely a nod to his Irish heritage, but the tree—whose branches she could see stretching down from his shoulder—she was curious about what that meant.

"And you are spending too much time thinking about him," she admonished herself.

She shouldn't be thinking about him at all. She should just focus on congratulating herself for saying nothing stupid. At least she hadn't cried and demanded answers for the night he had completely laid waste to her every feeling.

"How did it go?"

Sabrina turned and saw her sister-in-law, Lindy, come in. People would be forgiven for thinking that she and Lindy were actually biological sisters. In fact, they looked much more alike than Sabrina and her younger sister Beatrix did.

Like Sabrina, Lindy had long, straight blond hair. Bea, on the other hand, had freckles all over her face and a wild riot of reddish-brown curls that resisted taming almost as strongly as the youngest Leighton sibling herself did.

That was another thing Sabrina and Lindy had in common. They were predominantly tame. At least, they kept things as together as they possibly could on the surface.

"Fine."

"You didn't savage him with a cheese knife?"

"Lindy," Sabrina said, "please. This is dry-clean only." She waved her hand up and down, indicating her dress.

"I don't know what your whole issue is with him…"

Because no one spoke of it. Lindy had married Sabrina's brother after the unpleasantness. It was no secret that Sabrina and her father were estranged—even if it was a brittle, quiet estrangement. But unless Damien had told Lindy the details—and Sabrina doubted he knew all of them—her sister-in-law wouldn't know the whole story.

"I don't have an issue with him," Sabrina said. "I knew him thirteen years ago. That has nothing to do with now. It has nothing to do with this new venture for the winery. Which I am on board with one hundred percent." It was true. She was.

"Well," Lindy said, "that's good to hear."

She could tell that Lindy didn't believe her. "It's going to be fine. I'm looking forward to this." That was also true. Mostly. She was looking forward to expanding Grassroots. Looking forward to helping build the winery and making it into something that was truly theirs. So that her parents could no longer shout recriminations about Lindy stealing something from the Leighton family.

Eventually, they would make the winery so much more successful that most of it would be theirs.

And if her own issues with her parents were tangled up in all of this, then…that was just how it was.

Sabrina wanted it all to work, and work well. If for no other reason than to prove to Liam Donnelly that she was no longer the seventeen-year-old girl whose world he'd wrecked all those years ago.

In some ways, Sabrina envied the tangible ways in which Lindy had been able to exact revenge on Damien. Of course, Sabrina's relationship with Liam wasn't anything like a ten-year marriage ended by infidelity. She gritted her teeth. She did her best not to think about Liam. About the past. Because it hurt. Every damn time it hurt. It didn't matter if it should or not.

But now that he was back in Copper Ridge, now

that she sometimes just happened to run into him, it was worse. It was harder not to think about him.

Him and the grand disaster that had happened after.

* * * * *

Look for CHRISTMASTIME COWBOY,
available from Maisey Yates and HQN Books
wherever books are sold.

COMING NEXT MONTH FROM

HARLEQUIN
Desire

Available December 5, 2017

#2557 HIS SECRET SON
The Westmoreland Legacy • by Brenda Jackson
The SEAL who fathered Bristol's son died a hero's death...or so she
was told. But now Coop is back and vowing to claim his child! Her
son deserves to know his father, so Bristol must find a way to fight
temptation...and keep her heart safe.

#2558 BEST MAN UNDER THE MISTLETOE
Texas Cattleman's Club: Blackmail • by Jules Bennett
Planning a wedding with the gorgeous, sexy best man would have been a
lot easier if he weren't Chelsea Hunt's second-worst enemy. Gabe Walsh
is furious that the sins of his uncle have also fallen on him, but soon his
desire to prove his innocence turns into the desire to make her his!

#2559 THE CHRISTMAS BABY BONUS
Billionaires and Babies • by Yvonne Lindsay
Getting snowed in with his sexy assistant is difficult enough. But when
an abandoned baby is found in the stables, die-hard bachelor Piers may
find himself yearning for a family for Christmas...

#2560 LITTLE SECRETS: HIS PREGNANT SECRETARY
Little Secrets • by Joanne Rock
After a heated argument with his secretary turns sexually explosive,
entrepreneur Jager McNeill knows the right thing to do is propose...
because now she's carrying his child! But what will he do when she
won't settle for a marriage of convenience?

#2561 SNOWED IN WITH A BILLIONAIRE
Secrets of the A-List • by Karen Booth
Joy McKinley just *had* to be rescued by one of the wealthiest, sexiest
men she's ever met. Especially when she's hiding out in someone
else's house under a name that isn't hers. But when they get snowed in
together, can their romance survive the truth?

#2562 BABY IN THE MAKING
Accidental Heirs • by Elizabeth Bevarly
Surprise heir Hannah Robinson will lose her fortune if she doesn't get
pregnant. Enter daredevil entrepreneur Yeager Novak...and the child
they'll make together! Opposites attract on this baby-making adventure,
but will that be enough to turn their pact into a real romance?

HDCNM1117

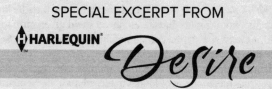
Laramie stared at Bristol. "You were pregnant?"

"Yes," she said in a soft voice. "And you're free to order a paternity test if you need to verify that my son is yours."

He had a son? It took less than a second for his emotions to go from shock to disbelief. "How?"

She lifted a brow. "Probably from making love almost nonstop for three solid days."

They had definitely done that. Although he'd used a condom each and every time, he knew there was always a possibility that something could go wrong.

"And where is he?" he asked.

"At home."

Where the hell was that? It bothered him how little he knew about the woman who'd just announced she'd given birth to his child. At least she'd tried contacting him to let him know. Some women would not have done so.

If his child had been born nine months after their holiday fling, that meant he would have turned two in September. While Laramie was in a cell, somewhere in the world, Bristol had been giving life.

To his child.

Emotions Laramie had never felt before suddenly bombarded him with the impact of a Tomahawk missile. He was a parent, which meant he had to think about someone other than himself. He wasn't sure how he felt about that. But then, wasn't he used to taking care of others as a member of his SEAL team?

She nodded. "I'm not asking you for anything Laramie, if that's what you're thinking. I just felt you had a right to know about the baby."

She wasn't asking him for anything? Did she not know her bold declaration that he'd fathered her child demanded everything?

"I want to see him."

"You will. I would never keep Laramie from you."

"You named him Laramie?" Even more emotions swamped him. Her son—their son—had his name?

She hesitated. "Yes."

Then he asked, "So, what's your reason for giving yourself my last name, as well?"

Don't miss
HIS SECRET SON
by New York Times *bestselling author Brenda Jackson,*
available December 2017
wherever Harlequin® Desire books and ebooks are sold.

www.Harlequin.com

HDEXP1117

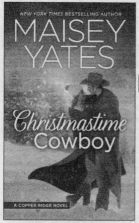

LOVE
Harlequin romance?

Join our Harlequin community to share your thoughts and connect with other romance readers!

Be the first to find out about promotions, news, and exclusive content!

Sign up for the Harlequin e-newsletter and download a free book from any series at
www.TryHarlequin.com

CONNECT WITH US AT:

Harlequin.com/Community

 Facebook.com/HarlequinBooks

Twitter.com/HarlequinBooks

Instagram.com/HarlequinBooks

Pinterest.com/HarlequinBooks

ReaderService.com

 HARLEQUIN®

ROMANCE WHEN YOU NEED IT

Love the Harlequin book you just read?

Your opinion matters.

Review this book on your favorite book site, review site, blog or your own social media properties and share your opinion with other readers!

Be sure to connect with us at:
Harlequin.com/Newsletters
Facebook.com/HarlequinBooks
Twitter.com/HarlequinBooks